THE LIGHTNING OF AUGUST

The Lightning
of August

JORGE IBARGÜENGOITIA

Translated by
Irene del Corral

Chatto & Windus
LONDON

Published in 1986 by
Chatto & Windus Ltd
40 William IV Street
London WC2N 4DF

British Library Cataloguing in Publication Data

Ibargüengoitia, Jorge
The lightning of August.
I. Title
863[F]   PQ7298.19.B3

ISBN 0–7011–3950–1
ISBN 0–7011–3951–X Pbk

Originally published in Mexico as
Los Relampagos de Agosto.

Published by arrangement with the estate of
Jorge Ibargüengoitia

This work is a novel. Any similarity to actual persons or events is
purely coincidental.

Printed and bound in Great Britain by
Redwood Burn Limited,
Trowbridge, Wiltshire

Explanatory Note

(for readers unversed in Mexican history)

In the thirty years of his widely censured reign, Porfirio Díaz built up a military establishment and an army three or four times the size of today's, which paraded every Independence Day to the cheers of the people. The officers went to France to learn *le cran* and to Germany to learn whatever it was the Prussians knew in those days. At the conclusion of the Boer War, Díaz hired two or three of their generals to come and make fools of themselves in Coahuila. The Mexican infantry was the first to use an automatic rifle, the Swiss-made Mondragon. A few are still being used in the Sunday-morning martial exercises of the eighteen-year-olds in compulsory military training.

All this collapsed with the Constitutional Revolution of 1913. The officers educated in France and Germany, the Boer generals, and the infantry with their shiny Mondragons—all were literally pulverized by a revolutionary army under Obregón, a farmer; under Pancho Villa, a cattle-rustler; under Venustiano Carranza, a politician; and I don't know what Pablo González was in real life, but he had every appearance of being a practicing notary public. These men were, in a manner of speaking, the fathers of a new military generation whose main concern, between 1915 and 1930, was self-annihilation. In Celaya, Obregón defeated Pancho Villa, who still had faith in cavalry charges; Pablo González ordered the assassination of Emiliano Zapata; Venustiano Carranza was shot down when he was running for his life; it has never been proven whether this was by direct order or merely with the blessings of Obregón who, in turn, died when a young Catholic drawing teacher pumped seven bullets into him. Pancho Villa met his end in an ambush prepared by a man who wanted to settle some unfinished business. Traces of arsenic were discovered in the intestines of Benjamín Hill, Secretary of War and the Navy; Lucio Blanco's body was found floating in the Rio Grande; General Diéguez died by mistake in a battle he had nothing to do with; General Serrano was shot with his staff on the road to Cuernavaca and General Arnulfo R. Gómez was shot with his in the State of Veracruz. Fortunato Maycotte who, according to a popular ballad, spotted Pancho Villa's troops from a tower where he was standing beside Obregón, was killed by Obregón's own men. General Murguía led troops from across the border and penetrated a thousand kilometers into Mexico without being discovered; when he was discovered, he was shot. Et cetera, et cetera, et cetera.

The great purges were not entirely effective. As late as 1938, there were still over two hundred generals on active duty. Of these, more than forty held the rank of Major General—division commanders—although the enlisted force was insufficient to compose even three divisions.

The problem was solved by the Retirement Pension Law. Today, the Mexican Army has the number of generals it needs; the rest are buried, retired, or in business.

THE LIGHTNING
OF AUGUST

Chapter I

Where to begin? It's nobody's business where I was born or who my parents were, or how many years I went to school, or why I was appointed the President's Private Secretary. However, I want to make it perfectly clear that I was not born in a dirt-floor hut, as Fatty Artajo claims, and my mother was not a prostitute, as some have hinted; nor is it true that I never entered a schoolroom, but finished the sixth grade (with praise from my teachers, as a matter of fact). As to the post of Private Secretary to the President of the Republic, it was offered to me in recognition of my personal merits, which include impeccable etiquette that invariably rouses admiration and envy, unwavering honesty that has, on occasion, gotten me into trouble with the police, alert intelligence, and, above all, a pleasing personality that many envious people find insufferable.

Suffice it to say that when I was thirty-eight, just at the time my luck ran out, with the rank of Brigadier General, in command of the Forty-fifth Cavalry Regiment, I was enjoying the peaceful delights of my home, in the company of my beloved wife (Matilde) and our numerous offspring, when I received a letter I have kept to this day. It read . . .
(It should be mentioned that all this happened in 1928 in a city that, to avoid guesswork, I will call Vieyra, capital of the State of the same name: Vieyra, Vieyra.) As I started to say, the letter read:

Dear Lupe:

As you probably know from the papers, I won the election by a landslide. I think this is one of the great triumphs of the Revolution. You might say I've struck it rich again. Come to Mexico City to see me as soon as you can. I want you to be my Private Secretary.

> [Signed]
> Marcos González
> Major General

Naturally, I immediately withdrew from my spouse's arms, said good-bye to the kids, left the tranquillity of my hearthside, and went to the casino to celebrate.

Don't think that it was my promotion that made me so happy (though you must admit it's a far cry from Commander of the Forty-fifth Regiment to Secretary to the President), for I have always prided myself on indifference to personal gain. No sir! What really pleased me was that my qualities were being officially rewarded at last. I wired González the reply customary in these cases, one that's always heartfelt: IN THIS NEW POST I WILL BE BETTER ABLE TO COLLABORATE IN CARRYING OUT THE GOALS OF THE REVOLUTION.

Of all the generals in the Nation's army at the time, what made González pick me as his Private Secretary? Very simple, because of my merits, as I mentioned before, and also because he owed me two favors. First of all, it was entirely González's fault that we lost the battle at Sante Fé; he was supposed to advance with the cavalry brigade as soon as I'd cleared Santiago Ridge of rifle fire, and he never did. Either he was scared or he forgot, and they slaughtered us and I was blamed for it. But since I'm such a good judge of character, I knew he'd get ahead someday, so I kept my mouth shut. I took all the reprimands, and things like that earn gratitude. The second favor is a secret and I will take it to my grave.

Getting back to my story, then, I celebrated my appointment, though not as wildly as some later said. Oh yes, champagne has always been one of my weaknesses, and there was plenty of it on that occasion; but when Deputy Solís shot at Colonel Medina, it was over a question of jealousy I had nothing to do with, and when Eulalia Arozamena jumped out of the window stark naked, I didn't push her, but was only trying to stop her. Anyway, both Colonel Medina and Miss Arozamena survived, so the whole thing boils down to the kind of trivial gossip that's been spread about me all my life, just because some people envy my nice manners and refined politeness.

At ten the next morning, I got on the train for Mexico City, and after taking off the belt that held my pearl-handled pistol and hanging it on a hook, I settled into a comfortable Pullman seat.

I'm not much of a reader, but whenever I travel I usually leaf through a newspaper. That's what I was doing when General Macedonio Gálvez came into the car; he was wearing a ten-gallon hat and smoking a cigar, nonchalant as you please, as if he'd never been kicked out of the country. He pretended not to see me, but I stopped him as he went by and said:

"Where are you going, Macedonio? Don't you remember me anymore?" I call him by his first name because we were once in the same outfit.

He acted as if he hadn't seen me until then, and looked surprised.

"Of course, Lupe." And then we embraced and all that. We sat down facing each other, and that was when I noticed how seedy he looked and that there was nothing new about him except the cigar.

Macedonio is one of the worst examples of rotten military luck I've ever known: in the Battle of Buenavista, in 1917, he had González running like a scared rabbit, and then he went around bragging, telling everybody he'd whipped González; and then in 1920, González is President for the first time, and he's inaugurated, and his very first official act is to throw Macedonio out of the country.

That morning he told me he'd been living in Amarillo, Texas, for eight years, but he got so bored, and things went so badly for him there, that he was coming back to Mexico, even if only to get himself killed (and that was probably just what would happen because, as we all know, González had been elected again). And he told me the story everybody who comes back to Mexico without permission tells: the one about his brother being at death's door. Then he asked me not to mention that I'd seen him because he was traveling incognito. I replied indignantly that he was insulting me by even suggesting such a thing because I have a reputation for kindness, loyalty to my friends, and generosity to people in unfortunate circumstances. No sooner were these words out of my mouth than he took me up on them and asked for three hundred pesos. I turned him down. Not because I didn't have the money, but because East is East and West is West, but a loan is something else. I decided the least I could do was buy his lunch, and he accepted. I got up from my seat, put the gun and belt into the little hammock, the newspaper on top of them, buttoned my jacket, and we went to the dining car together.

We had a couple of drinks and then ordered a big meal. (I didn't tell him about my appointment because I don't like to boast. Besides there are times when things don't work out—like that time.) But to continue: While we were eating, the train stopped at X, a big town, and when they were calling ''All aboard'' Macedonio got up, said he had to go to the men's room, left the dining car, and I went on eating; the train started again, and I continued eating; I finished eating and Macedonio still wasn't back; and I ordered a cognac, and still no sign of him; and I paid the bill and he still wasn't back; I walked to my car and when I reached my seat, I saw . . . Of course! By now you've guessed what it was I saw, because you'd have to be as big a jackass as I was not to figure it out: Instead of going to the men's room, Macedonio had gone for my pistol and, when the train stopped, he got off. On several occasions in my lifetime I've come up against situations that have left me appalled at human wickedness. This was one of them.

I wired the X Garrison from the next station, ordering them to execute Macedonio if they could catch him, but it was useless . . . well, it wasn't so useless, or rather, it's a good thing it was, as you'll see in due course.

I got hardly any sleep that night, I was so angry, and when the new day came, I had no idea that within a few hours my military career would receive a blow from which it would never recover.

They must have put the newspapers on board at the last stop. While I was shaving in the men's room, I heard somebody passing by say ''The old man died!'' I paid no attention and was still shaving when the conductor came in with a newspaper. The headline read ''GENERAL GONZÁLEZ DEAD OF APOPLEXY!!!'' And there was a picture of González, the big boss, the hero of a thousand battles, the President-Elect, Mexico's leader . . . who had just appointed me his Private Secretary.

I don't know why or how I got onto the platform, my face still covered with lather, but from there I had a view of a spectacle that seemed particularly appropriate to the moment: a row of men at the foot of a fence attending to their physiological needs.

Chapter II

In this chapter I will reveal the manner in which ever-fickle Lady Luck dealt me the second treacherous blow of that day, a day that was ill-omened indeed, not only for my military career, but also for Mexico, my beloved country on whose behalf I have endured, without complaint, so much pain and so many sleepless nights.

As soon as I got off the train, I sent for the stationmaster; upon seeing my handsome uniform and hearing my tone of authority and my explanation that there was a National Emergency, he quickly offered me the use of the telephone in his private office; I called Germán Trenza, who was a good friend of mine at the time.

"The old man went and died on us, Lupe!" he wailed, almost sobbing. He was supposed to be the new Secretary of Agriculture and Development.

"What are we going to do?"

"Go to the wake. We can figure out the next step there."

I hung up. Then I ordered the stationmaster to see to it that my bags were delivered to the Cosmopolita Hotel and I took a Model T taxi to Trenza's house.

I found him putting on his boots with the help of Camila, his mistress. The house I'm talking about was actually what nowadays might be called a "love nest." Trenza's official home, where his legal wife lived, was in Tampico, where he

7

was regional Commander for the whole State of Tamaulipas.

While Camila curled his mustache, he gave me a quick rundown of the situation: González's death had plunged the Nation into chaos; the only political figure of any prominence just then was President Vidal Sánchez, but since his reelection would be unconstitutional, it was up to us to find someone to fill the office and guarantee respect for the sacred principles of the Revolution and for the legitimate demands of all political parties.

Germán's automobile was parked in front of the house. We got in and as we sped toward González's home, he said:

"There's something else we have to make sure of when we pick the next President, Lupe." (Germán drove his powerful Packard expertly.) "Whoever it is will have to give us his word that he'll keep the promises the old man made us."

"He'd just made me his Private Secretary!"

It occurred to me then that although I had no political ambitions whatsoever, there might still be a chance for official recognition of my merits, even though my ex-boss, dear to me as a father, was gone.

González's house was on Londres Street, across from the Spanish Embassy. A column of troops representing all three branches of the armed forces, under Fatty Artajo's orders, was to pay final military honors; it stretched for several kilometers; the mourners' double-parked automobiles lined the side streets all the way to Chapultepec Park. The city was completely paralyzed. Scowling faces could be glimpsed peering between the slats of shutters; children, unaware that the Leader's death was a calamity for their country, scampered happily among crepe-hung drums. The entire Nation mourned.

To this day I don't know how we managed to get into the house; we elbowed a path between bureaucrats, representatives of labor organizations and farmers' groups, distinguished members of the Diplomatic Corps, Cabinet hopefuls, Cabinet members, fellow officers of the deceased, his friends and relatives. At last we reached the side of the distraught widow, who clutched us to her bosom like long-lost brothers.

The sister of my beloved, too-soon-departed Chief led us to the Chinese Salon, where the coffin had been placed. An honor guard was standing at attention when we arrived: Vidal Sánchez in a Prince Albert, a wide satin sash with the colors of the flag across his breast; Fatty Artajo in dress uniform; Juan Valdivia, who apparently hadn't had time to change into black because he was still wearing his green gabardine suit; and finally . . . none other than Eulalio Pérez. . . .

The sister nudged us toward the casket.

"Just look at him. He looks like he's asleep."

I swear I've never seen a corpse so disfigured.

As I was leaving the Chinese Salon, the widow beckoned to me, as if she wanted to talk to me in private. I followed her all the way to the basement pantry. She stopped there.

"Do you know what his last words were?"

Naturally, I replied that I didn't. Then she made one of the most astonishing disclosures I've ever heard:

" 'I want Lupe to have my gold watch.' He meant you."

I can't begin to describe the effect these words had on me. His last thoughts were of me! My eyes burned with tears. But then she told me something that would later bring awful repercussions.

"I wish I could give it to you because I . . ." Then she told me how dearly she loved her husband and all that. "But, you know what? It's been stolen!"

"Who took it?" I demanded indignantly.

Then she explained that she'd put the watch on the

nightstand beside the bed and that the only person who'd gone into the room (to get González's sword) had been Pérez. I mean the Pérez we all know: Eulalio Pérez. I'd be willing to swear under oath before any judge—even the Divine—that Marcos González's widow told me that Eulalio Pérez had stolen the watch bequeathed to me by her husband with his dying breath.

Moved by a strong urge to knock the teeth of the aforementioned individual down his throat (as some might put it crudely), I started for the stairs. But the widow stopped me.

I suppose I ought to add an explanation here. I'm talking about Marcos González's real widow. In other words, the one who's officially recognized as legitimate: Soledad Espino González. Other ladies who have been called widows of General González belong to another, greatly inferior class of society.

"Where are you going?"

I told her what I intended to do. She pleaded with me to wait for some other occasion.

"It's hard enough to have lost a husband," she said, "without having all these scenes."

I knew what she meant. Like so many others devoted to the hazardous, though glorious, military life, Marcos González had been obliged to accept the services of several women and had fathered offspring by some of them. Soledad confided that four women in widows' weeds had arrived at the wake with no fewer than a dozen unrecognized heirs in tow. (They were, by the way, blamed for the disappearance of some silverware and Venetian crystal.) It was a very uncomfortable situation, for obvious reasons. Always the gentleman, I acceded to her wishes and promised that I wouldn't make another scene in her home.

On my way through the corridors back to the wake, I literally ran into Vidal Sánchez, who grabbed me by the arm and said:

"Come by the office, Lupe. I have to talk to you before you leave the city." His very words. Then he went away and before I had a chance to reply, I watched in horror as the President of the Republic (Vidal Sánchez, whose high position lent him dignity even if he was a heartless murderer) went to stand beside the crook Pérez, who'd just stolen the last memento of my beloved leader; they exchanged a few words, then together approached the Ambassador of the United States. I'm positive I saw Jefferson nod in agreement to something they told him.

I turned my head, trying to find something less impure to look at, just in time to spot a senator pocketing a porcelain figurine. In despair, I returned to the Chinese Salon and had been standing at attention for a quarter of an hour when Germán Trenza appeared. He sidled up to me and whispered mysteriously:

"The boys are in the dining room." Then he went away.

I followed him to the mansion's large, dark dining room (an exact replica of the one in Chapultepec Castle) where my old army buddies had gathered to sample the last bottles of General González's favorite cognac.

Even in the dimly lit room I could make out the imposing figure of Fatty Artajo in dress uniform. Standing around him were Germán Trenza, Canalejo, Juan Valdivia, Anastasio Rodríguez, and Augusto Corona.

I closed the door behind me and Trenza rushed to prop a chair under the knob. Everyone there greeted me with friendly respect. As soon as Germán and I were seated, Juan Valdivia got up and started to speak.

"Comrades!" (In his student days, he'd won a State-wide oratory championship.) "We have gathered here in sadness, apprehension and distress, to decide the posture we will assume, the words we will believe, the course we will follow, in these moments of violent transition—in these moments when the Nation, still reeling from the shock caused by the untimely demise of our dear General González, contemplates a clouded future, filled with apocalyptical phantasms.'' Et cetera, et cetera.

He went on in this vein for quite a while, and then yielded the floor to Artajo; Fatty was the most important man there, partly because he was a heavyweight, but maybe also because he commanded seven thousand men and four artillery regiments. (He was holding a copy of the Constitution in his hand.)

''As we all know,'' said Fatty from where he was sitting, ''our country's Constitution provides that in the event the President of the Republic dies, the Secretary of the Interior automatically assumes the office.''

We all burst into cheers and applause for Valdivia, who was Secretary of the Interior. Somebody proposed a toast; but Augusto Corona, the Chameleon, raised his hand and said:

''Just a moment, gentlemen.'' Turning to Fatty, he added, ''I'm afraid you're mistaken, General.''

Fatty was visibly annoyed but, with a show of chivalry, asked the Chameleon to explain, which he did as follows, more or less:

''The section of the Constitution on which you have undoubtedly based your interesting remarks, General, deals with the death of a President during his term of office, and General González was only President-Elect. This section would apply if the deceased were General Vidal Sánchez, which is not the case, unfortunately.''

There was a silence, broken by Fatty Artajo:

''Oh, well, it's the same thing.''

"No, it isn't, General," the Chameleon replied. "Read Clause N to us aloud, if you would."

As it turned out, Clause N said something entirely different: Upon the death of a President-Elect, Congress would appoint an Acting President who would be charged with the duty of calling and supervising new elections.

Another silence followed. This one was gloomy because it would be one thing to have Valdivia as Acting President (he could be trusted), but it would be quite another matter to be at the mercy of the Chamber of Deputies, who are afraid of their own shadows and would listen to the first voice of authority that happened to come along.

"I suggest," said Canalejo, the Jinx of the Mexican Army, "that our colleague, Anastasio Rodríguez, himself a Deputy, present a motion in the Chamber that Clause N be annulled because it's unsuitable."

"Why is it unsuitable?" asked Anastasio. This particular Deputy was so shy he'd never opened his mouth in the Chamber. I can't understand how he ever make Brigadier General.

"For the simple reason that it doesn't do us a bit of good," Trenza explained calmly.

Then I spoke up. I remember distinctly that I said only this:

"We'll all be sitting in the gallery, Anastasio. You'll have our full moral support." And not, as Fatty Artajo has reported in his *Memoirs*, "We'll surround the Chamber with our troops and force the Deputies to set aside the Constitution because it's unsuitable." This is libel, unbecoming to an officer of the Mexican Army. In the first place, my troops (that is, the Forty-fifth Cavalry) were in Vieyra, Vieyra; in the second place, I have always held the Constitution, our Magna Charta, to be one of the Nation's greatest glories, and for that reason, it should never be set aside; in the third

place, I've always known that the Deputies are a bunch of
idiots and you don't need any troops to make them do anything you want them to.

After I said these words, I mean the ones about the gallery
and moral support, not the ones about the troops, the Chameleon said:

"Gentlemen, we must bear in mind that any attempt to
annul Clause N will bring an uproar from public opinion."

Germán Trenza, Hero of the Battle of Salamanca, Defender of Parral, broke in to tell the Chameleon, in no uncer-
tain terms, what he could do with public opinion.

We all applauded this manly rejoinder; then the Jinx made
the following suggestion:

"We could take out Clause N and put in something like
this: 'When the President-Elect dies, the President still in
power is automatically replaced by the Secretary of the Interior.' "

There were shouts of "Down with Vidal Sánchez!" and
"Valdivia for President!" and just as we were warming up
to our celebration, we noticed that Valdivia was standing,
waiting for silence, so he could make another speech:

"Comrades! My heart melts in the onslaught of the thousand conflicting emotions that this occasion . . ." He
talked about his gratitude to us, about his sense of duty,
about the Constitution and Venustiano Carranza and said
we'd better not rock the boat, because of the Nation and the
blood of her sons and all that. To make a long story short, he
said everything could be worked out quite easily. He ended
with some ideas that gave us food for thought:

"Who chooses the next President? The President in
power. And who'll have the power? The Acting President.
And who appoints the Acting President? The Chamber of
Deputies. And, finally, who controls the Chamber? President Vidal Sánchez! Well, then, it's simple. We merely

have to make a deal with Vidal Sánchez to put Fatty Artajo in as Acting President. Fatty sets up and supervises the election, and yours truly will win by an overwhelming majority.''

More applause. We were all in complete agreement and made a date to meet at the Earthly Paradise Restaurant the next day. Over lunch we'd work out the details of how to oblige Vidal Sánchez to accept our demands that were, after all, in full accord with the loftiest principles of the Mexican Revolution.

Once we'd gotten business out of the way, a great feeling of fellowship descended on us; we drank toasts to one another, we shook hands, we embraced, and, of course, there were a few speeches. The room was flooded with joy. A sharp knock on the door brought us back to grim reality; the funeral cortege was about to get under way, to deposit the onetime Leader of Men in his Final Resting Place.

Chapter III

For purely literary reasons having to do with rhythm and space, I failed to keep the promise made in the first paragraph of the last chapter: to "reveal the manner in which ever-fickle Lady Luck dealt me the second treacherous blow of that day." In this chapter I intend to fulfill my commitment.

Everyone knows that all funeral processions move slowly. But when a cortege is escorted by a whole army corps, it's even worse. By the time we reached the cemetery, it was dark and a torrent of rain was beating down on the city.

Many of the generals disputed the honor of being pallbearers for their former leader, but since it was slippery underfoot, they reluctantly yielded this privilege to a platoon from the Sixteenth Battalion.

The downpour and late hour notwithstanding, Vidal Sánchez insisted on delivering the farewell speech he'd brought. It was the usual one, the one that begins, "You are departing this world, illustrious leader . . .," et cetera, and one of the craftiest pieces of oratory I've ever heard. How did he have the nerve to say "cherished friend"? When he got himself surrounded at El Nopalito and General González went to bail him out, it wasn't out of friendship, but because all supply lines would have been cut if El Nopalito was taken; and later, when Sánchez picked González to succeed

17

him in the Presidency, that wasn't out of affection either, but because he had no choice; it was a High Policy decision. Besides, how could he say "you are leaving us in darkness" when he knew perfectly well what he had to do? And what about that part, "We, the brothers you leave behind, will carry on for you and see to it that the democratic process is respected"? Even as he was saying it, he'd made up his mind to stab us in the back and make the democratic process the laughingstock it still is today. Vidal Sánchez was a rat. He is a rat.

As I patiently listened to this gibberish, it was my misfortune to need a handkerchief, to reach into my jacket pocket and to feel, with a shudder of rage, the absence of my pearl-handled pistol. My jaws clenched as I recalled the loss suffered at the hands of Macedonio Gálvez, and a thirst for revenge came over me. This thought led to another: the gold watch and Pérez. I noted with disgust that he was standing only a few steps away from me with his ridiculous bald spot, his sissy mustache, his revolting double chin, and that pear-shaped body wrapped in a dripping suit. If I had my gun, I think I'd have killed him then and there and performed a service to the Nation. As luck had it, my fate was to be less glorious and Mexico more unfortunate.

When the speech finally came to an end, we disbanded and I lost my way among the tombstones. I wandered around, desperately searching for the exit (not because a pitch-black cemetery scares me, but because I had no intention of spending the night in so uncomfortable a place). Then I saw the light of a lantern in the distance and hurried toward it. When he heard my footsteps, the man stopped and shone the light in my direction. "Holy mackerel!" As soon as I heard his voice, I knew it was Pérez, the crook.

"Oh! It's you, Lupe!" The hypocrite invited me to walk with him. I approached him wordlessly, my heart filled with a thousand conflicting emotions. We took a few steps. Then I asked him, "What did you do with the watch?"

"Which watch?"

"The one you stole!"

"I never stole any watch, my friend." He said this with a perfectly straight face, as if he'd really never stolen a watch.

The lantern showed a newly opened grave. I couldn't stand it anymore. I couldn't stand his gall, his dishonesty, his cowardice. With a rapid movement of my well-exercised muscles, I shoved him into the hole. And he, who'd been a pen-pusher all his life and had a flabby body, plummeted into the slimy mud with a splash. The lantern went out; I guess it sank. I started to walk again, groping my way along and turning a deaf ear to Pérez, who was screaming stupidly:

"Lupe, help me! Why did you push me? What's eating you, you rotten bum?. . ." Et cetera. The insults became increasingly uncouth. I'd have killed him if I'd had something to do it with.

So this was Lady Luck's second treacherous blow because the very next day the Chamber of Deputies met in emergency session and named the Acting President: Eulalio Pérez.

Chapter IV

It took me a good half-hour to get out of the cemetery. My friends had left by then; the Japanese ambassador kindly offered to take me to the Cosmopolita Hotel in his Rolls-Royce. When we got there, I thanked the gracious oriental, went into the hotel, then ordered the manager to have a hot bath prepared and to send a good dinner and a bottle of Martell cognac to my room. I wanted to take every possible precaution against catching cold; I had to be in condition for the coming political struggle.

I was pleased because I knew I'd punished someone who really deserved it and, at the same time, I'd kept my promise to Mrs. González. The punishment had been both swift and discreet. But, oh, what heartaches lay in store for me the following day!

I slept soundly after my bath, dinner, and cognac, and the first thing I did in the morning was get a Smith and Wesson, thinking it might come in handy.

There were several private dining rooms in the Earthly Paradise. The maître d' led me upstairs to the one reserved for us. Fatty Artajo had been the first to arrive; he was alone in the room when I got there. We ordered a bottle of excellent *mezcal*, with the idea of sipping it as we waited for the others.

He was excited.

"I've found a treasure!" he exclaimed. It was a certified

copy (and it must have been certified a long time before, because nobody would have dared certify anything that mentioned the President) of a commission as Colonel in the Infantry of the infamous Huerta government; it was issued to one Vidal Sánchez who, of course, wasn't necessarily the same one . . . or maybe he was because, as I've already said, he was crafty. "This little piece of paper could mean my Acting Presidency, Lupe," Fatty gloated.

The Jinx and the Chameleon came in then. They couldn't stand each other but now, since they'd left the funeral together and spent the night drinking and having a good time, they were very chummy. When he heard about the commission, the Jinx slapped his forehead as if he'd just remembered something.

"Of course!" There was a colonel by that name who surrendered to me at the Battle of Santa Rosa!"

"But I thought you told me you were with Pablo's troops!" I protested. The Jinx was from Monterrey and it was highly unlikely that he'd have gone clear across the country to take part in the Battle of Santa Rosa. Besides, if he had, we wouldn't have won because, as everyone knows, every single campaign he was ever involved in had been a complete failure. That's why we called him "The Jinx of the Mexican Army."

But he swore up and down that he'd been at Santa Rosa and gave some very peculiar explanations: that he'd joined up with Venustiano Carranza and I don't know what else. Just then, Juan Valdivia rushed in with something much more sensational: some letters Vidal Sánchez had written saying he wasn't sure if the Revolution was necessary or even desirable and questioning where it might lead. This was marvelous because the letters were signed and there could be no question that they were authentic—samples of his signature were everywhere—even on two-peso bills.

We were holding three aces: the commission, the surrender, and the letters, and we had Vidal Sánchez exactly where we wanted him. Fatty Artajo was already Acting President as far as we were concerned. We never suspected that a few short hours earlier, the Chamber of Deputies had yielded, like a harlot, to the beastly demands of the Tyrant!

The first hint of trouble was brought by Germán Trenza.

"I heard they called a session of the Chamber of Deputies."

We ran to the telephone and I asked to be connected with Anastasio Rodríguez who, as I've mentioned, was a Deputy.

"Anastasio isn't here," his wife told me. "He didn't come home all night."

I called the Chamber and asked whether there'd been a session.

"Yes, sir, there was an emergency session," the janitor replied. But there was no way I could get anything out of him about what was going on. And there was no one else around who could give us any information.

We simply had to track down Anastasio, our only contact with the Congress. There's an important lesson to be learned from this episode: If we'd had more members of Congress as our friends, on our side, it would have been a different story. That's why Congress shouldn't be sneered at; every once in a while, because of a few weak points in our Magna Charta, the destiny of the Nation falls into their hands.

I called the Harem Baths and again asked for Anastasio.

"He's in the steam room," I was told. When they heard this, my companions started to swear. "Tell him General José Guadalupe Arroyo is on the line. Tell him to come to the telephone at once."

Before long, Anastasio was assuring me he'd join us at the restaurant in a couple of minutes.

"Don't bother," I said. "Just tell us what happened at the Chamber."

"Which chamber?"

It was hopeless. I slammed down the receiver and called the newsroom of *El Mundo*. They refused to give me any information.

"The special edition is on the streets by now. Why don't you go out and buy a copy?"

We sent an aide for some newspapers. We returned to the dining room and sat around the table; we weren't hungry, we weren't thirsty, and no one felt like talking. All our excitement had vanished. We were beaten. We'd spent hours planning a battle that was lost before it ever started. Although we knew all this, the arrival of the newspaper brought the most nauseating moment of my life: "EULALIO PÉREZ NAMED ACTING PRESIDENT!"

I thought I'd die. The others, unaware of my mishap, started to work out a new plan of attack.

"We could kill Vidal Sánchez before his term ends; then Valdivia would become President," suggested Germán Trenza, the best strategist of the whole group.

"Remember this is July, Germán, and Pérez takes office in December. Five months won't give us enough time to do anything," said Valdivia, who was really very sensible. Credit where credit is due.

"It *would* be a tall order," Fatty added.

"Besides, we've got to think about public opinion," said the Chameleon, the only one who ever worried about things like that. Maybe that's why he's doing so well, even today.

Trenza was the first to notice the look on my face and asked, "What's the matter, Lupe?"

I told them my story, the one about the watch and the cemetery. Then they did something I'd never have expected of them. They advised me to apologize to Pérez.

"I refuse to apologize to a common thief," I said with dignity. "Besides, it would be embarrassing to Mrs. González."

They pointed out that Mrs. González was, after all, only the widow of an illustrious man—illustrious, but dead. I was upset but my decision was final and they couldn't make me change my mind.

Then Valdivia, who'd been silent all along, stood up and said:

"It will take a while for things to settle down. In the meantime, I think we have no choice but to pay a visit to the President of the Republic, General Vidal Sánchez, and congratulate him for his speedy, legitimate, and unselfish actions that will safeguard political order in the country."

I was shocked by the very idea, but all the others agreed!

I got to my feet and said:

"I absolutely refuse to call on that tyrant!"

They tried to calm me down and convince me it had to be done.

"We have to get into his good graces; later on we'll figure out how to deal with Pérez."

"I have no intention of ever dealing with Pérez." I added that they and I didn't make "we," and that I was ashamed I'd even taken part in their meetings.

They answered that if we weren't "we" and I was ashamed of having taken part in their meetings and I didn't intend to call on Vidal Sánchez or deal with Pérez, I had no further business there and I could go straight to . . . (my good manners do not allow me to be more specific).

In view of their inflexible attitude, I took my regulation cap and overcoat from the rack where they hung, put them on, and angrily left the Earthly Paradise.

Another unpleasant surprise awaited me at the Cosmopolita Hotel.

When I asked for my room key at the desk, the clerk handed me a black-bordered envelope and a small package wrapped in brown paper. I opened the envelope and took out a note in a woman's handwriting; it read:

Dear Lupe:

I'm sending you my late husband's watch. I found it in a dresser drawer. I didn't remember putting it there.

Give my love to Matilde.

Soledad E. González

Chapter V

For reasons that are surely obvious, I couldn't sleep that night; I drank a bottle of Martell to settle my nerves, but it didn't help. As I lay awake, I went so far as to toy with the idea of apologizing to Pérez, and even thought up an explanation of the cemetery incident that would save face for me and, up to a point, for Mrs. González who, after all, was the one who'd gotten me into this mess in the first place. I knew that if I went through with my plan, my friends would forgive me immediately.

But the scheme I'd worked out during the night vanished in the morning when a Presidential aide came to my room with orders for me to report to Vidal Sánchez at Chapultepec Castle at noon. I told him I'd be there and, as I ate breakfast at a café, I decided that even if Pérez hadn't stolen the watch in question, the punishment was well deserved anyway because he'd been a dishonest man all his life.

I read in the newspapers that my friends had gone to congratulate the President and that he'd told them, among other things, that Mexico had "surpassed the Caudillo phase" . . . a slap in the face for the Deceased.

I went shopping for some toys for my large family and for a few things Matilde had asked me to pick up for her while I was in Mexico City, and then I took a Model T taxi to Chapultepec Castle.

Vidal Sánchez had me ushered into his office so quickly that I suspected he had something up his sleeve. He did.

"You didn't come with the others who came to see me yesterday, Lupe." We'd known each other a long time, ever since I served under him in the disastrous Lechuga campaign. He was a tyrant of a boss and a god-awful strategist.

I told him I hadn't come with the others because of a bad cold, and that was practically the truth because it must have been a miracle that saved me from getting sick after the soaking I got at the cemetery.

"I want to be your friend, Lupe," he said. His very words. Then he added, "I know you're an honest man and I want your frank opinion of Eulalio."

With my characteristic civic courage, I said:

"The man doesn't have sufficient energy [I used different words], nobody likes him, and he's never been any good in the field. He's utterly incapable of setting up and carrying out a free election."

"Where did you get the idea anyone gives a damn about a free election?"

I was shocked by his indiscretion and reminded him of the sacrosanct principles of the Revolution. He replied:

"Do you know what would happen if there was a free election? Some bishop would win. One of the major goals of the Revolution was to reduce the power, the influence—and the wealth—of the Church. And what's been going on ever since we separated Church and State? You know as well as I that the Catholics have turned into fanatics. Now they even have their 'army,' the *Cristeros*, taking potshots at us every chance they get. You and I are true Revolutionaries, Lupe, and we know what's best for the country, believe me. But we're still in the minority. What we need at this moment is a strong Revolutionary government, not a free election!"

I didn't know what to say. He went on:

"To reach our goal—a Revolutionary government—we have to stick together. But union is impossible around a vigorous leader like you, like me, like González; what we need is somebody with no friends, no enemies, no following, no plans, no past, no future; in other words, a puppet. That's why I picked Eulalio."

I had to admit that made sense, and said so. Vidal changed the subject.

"I sent for you because I need your help. Can I count on you?"

I assured him that he could, as long as he asked nothing that might offend my moral ethics or my integrity as a Mexican Revolutionary officer.

"I don't trust Cenón Hurtado and suspect he's collaborating with the *Cristeros.*" Major General Cenón Hurtado was Regional Commander in the Vieyra zone. It was true he couldn't be trusted, but he couldn't possibly be in league with the *Cristeros* for the simple reason that there weren't any in Vieyra. Vidal Sánchez asked me, "How would you like to have his job?"

I said yes at once.

"I'll tell Melitón to take care of the details." Melitón Anguiano was Secretary of War and the Navy, another puppet.

So I left Chapultepec Castle that day with an assignment too big for my rank and, as time would tell, for my endurance. Soon afterward I learned that my erstwhile companions, by then enemies, that is Germán Trenza, Fatty Artajo, the Jinx, and the Chameleon, had lost control of their forces and were scattered all over the country: Artajo was sent to Chiapas, where there were no troops; Trenza to Quintana Roo, where there weren't even any people; the Jinx to Puruándiro, where he didn't know a soul; and the Chameleon to Pochutla, famous for an entire population of cutthroats. Only Anastasio and Juan Valdivia were allowed to keep their jobs. But what harm can a Deputy and a Secretary of the Interior do? They don't have any troops.

That's what they all got for going to congratulate someone they shouldn't have for his sound leadership and all that.

The following week, my promotion came through along with my appointment as Regional Commander assigned to Vieyra; this earned me the undying hatred of Cenón Hurtado, and he gave me a lot of trouble from then on.

Instead of doing what's always done in cases like this—transfer the former commander as far away as possible—they left Cenón on post under my orders and "recommended" that I appoint him my Chief of General Staff. This decision caused me untold grief.

For the next three months in my new job (and I had no expectation it would last any more than five because I knew that as soon as Pérez took office, he'd get rid of me in the most humiliating way he could think of), everything ran smoothly; I had the barracks of the Twenty-sixth Battalion painted, I demoted one of my officers for incompetence, and I got rid of the troop followers, who'd turned the post into a marketplace. But then "The Pereira Case" came up and from then on, every time my name was printed in *El Sol de Vieyra*, the local newspaper, it was preceded by the adjective "bloodthirsty." I will report here exactly what happened to demonstrate that my actions were completely justified.

It all began with a telegram I received from Melitón Anguiano:

HAVE REASON TO BELIEVE CATHOLIC PROPAGANDA BEING PRINTED IN VIEYRA STOP ENLIST COOPERATION OF CIVIL-

IAN AUTHORITIES AND TAKE ANY ACTION YOU CONSIDER
NECESSARY.

Well, I had the Secret Police investigate, and they learned
that Catholic propaganda was being printed at the Government Print Shop and stored in the stockroom of a grocery
store called El Puerto de Vigo, the property of one Agustín
Pereira, a Spanish subject. I led an infantry battalion to the
print shop, where several people were arrested; once the
prisoners were in custody, I drove to El Puerto de Vigo; it
was already surrounded by another infantry company. When
we approached the store, an officer came to my automobile
to report that the grocer refused to let him into the storeroom
because he didn't have a warrant. It was true; we'd forgotten
to get one from the judge.

"Tell the proprietor that the Regional Commander is here
in person, and that we have to search his storeroom!"

The captain carried out my orders and soon returned to inform me that Agustín Pereira had made some impolite remarks about how I'd come by my title. I got out of the
automobile and strode into the store. I'll confess I was quite
angry.

"Repeat to me what you said to the captain, if you dare!"
I commanded.

Agustín Pereira was mad, frothing at the mouth. Instead
of repeating his words, he picked up a sausage and hurled it
into my face. The captain had his pistol out of its holster, but
I didn't. I merely warned the wild Spaniard of the conse-
quences if he persisted in remaining silent. Without speaking, he pushed an enormous glass jar of pickled chilies off
the counter; it tipped, broke on the floor, and splashed all
over me. My soldiers arrested him at once. The man had
gone too far! I gave orders for a rapid trial and execution.
The command was carried out.

If Agustín Pereira had been a Mexican, that would have been the end of it, but he was a citizen of Spain, so there was an awful fuss, even though we later found the afore-mentioned propaganda that had, indeed, been printed on Government paper, with Government ink, and on the Government's own presses.

The newspapers had a field day attacking me, and if I hadn't had Vidal Sánchez's backing, I'd have lost my post.

In time, the storm blew over. On December 1, Pérez was sworn in as Acting President of the Republic. I prepared my resignation and sent it in because I didn't want to start any gossip. On December 3, the newspapers published the list of new Cabinet members: Vidal Sánchez had been named Secretary of War and the Navy. My resignation wasn't accepted.

Chapter VI

It was then that my second streak of bad luck started, and it became apparent that if Melitón Anguiano was a puppet and Eulalio Pérez was a puppet, I was a puppet too. All the strings, of course, were held by that crafty tyrant, Vidal Sánchez.

For many years the Vieyra sector had been a model of tranquillity thanks, among other things, to the iron hand of its military commanders; suddenly all hell broke loose. The *Cristeros* who, as I mentioned before, were conspicuously absent from Vieyra, started to pour in from the four bordering states. Why? Because my fellow officers decided to carry out operations against the outlaws. They were acting independently, none of them knowing that the same thing was happening at the same time in the other three states. *And they never informed me of their plans.*

When I saw that my area was starting to crawl with these fanatic ruffians, I wasted no time and called a meeting of my staff to work out a strategy to get rid of them. The first phase of our plan, consisting of a series of preliminary maneuvers (attacks and withdrawals, et cetera), worked like a dream and we soon had the troublemakers concentrated in the region of San Mateo Milpalta. The second phase was to stage a frontal attack with our two infantry battalions while the three cavalry regiments surrounded the enemy, cutting off their retreat. Our objective was to surprise the *Cristeros* and finish them off. The only problem was that every last man in our force would be needed for the maneuver, and the rest of the State would be left completely unprotected. I wired Mexico City, requesting reinforcements, and Vidal Sánchez answered: SEEK OUT AND CHASTISE THE ENEMY.

While this message was very clear about what I was supposed to do, it was terribly hazy as to what he intended to do. That is, whether or not I was going to get the reinforcements. In any case, I took it to be an order to take immediate action and a confirmation that he'd see to the rest—that is, protect my rear.

Leaving the Chief of the Secret Police in charge of a total force of sixteen of his own men and four sick soldiers, I moved out with all my troops toward San Mateo Milpalta, two days' march away. We had no radio equipment, so we decided there was no point in setting up General Headquarters. We split up into two columns: Cenón Hurtado took charge of the infantry and I led the cavalry. The plan was for him to begin his frontal attack on January 18, 1929 (a date that was to prove fateful) at eight o'clock in the morning, by which time my men would be deployed in the hills overlooking a canyon that was the enemy's most likely escape route.

After a day's forced march, we reached the assigned place, and my men took their positions. I held one regiment in reserve, ready for pursuit in case the enemy tried to get out in some other direction.

At dawn of the eighteenth, I ordered my men to their combat stations. All was in readiness for the annihilation of the *Cristeros*. But they didn't appear. Instead, the Chief of the Secret Police came riding from Vieyra to inform me that a handful of *Cristeros* had quietly strolled into town and taken a hostage—none other than the State Governor, Virgilio Urquiza.

A curse escaped my lips. My most brilliant campaign had gone, if I were to put it rather vulgarly, to pot. And all because Vidal Sánchez failed to protect my rear.

We had no choice but to negotiate with the *Cristeros*. These nitwits didn't know the first thing about the art of war but, nevertheless, held the upper hand. Fortunately, between us, Cenón Hurtado and I had more than four hundred of them cornered. We released them in exchange for the Governor, and they moved on to Apapátaro, to the dismay of the military commander there.

I had to appear in Mexico City to defend myself, to justify my performance before Vidal Sánchez, the very man responsible for the failure of the operation in the first place. There was to be a Board of Inquiry, but naturally he canceled that because he knew that if I was obliged to tell the whole story, he'd be the one who'd come out looking like a fool.

Governor Urquiza was furious and complained about my lack of experience, but Vidal sent for him and shut him up. I was sorry I hadn't gone ahead with my original plans; I should have let the *Cristeros* keep him to do with as they pleased. He was, after all, the most incompetent man ever to rule Vieyra, a State that had already suffered more than its fair share of martyrdom under its authorities.

I presented my resignation (the customary procedure in these cases); once again it was rejected. I went back to Vieyra and the whole incident was hushed up and soon forgotten.

Chapter VII

These events, as I've said, took place in January and February of 1929. In March, Pérez called for elections and the political battle was on.

The first bombshell was the publication of González's "Political Testament" (it wasn't learned until later that it was a forgery); it placed my former companions, enemies at the moment, in extremely good positions—especially Juan Valdivia.

The text of this document is immaterial, but it had the following results: Juan Valdivia resigned as Secretary of the Interior and was authorized by the Chamber of Deputies to run for the Presidency of the Republic. Fatty Artajo was reinstated as Commander of the Sonora sector, Germán Trenza went back to Tamaulipas to his old job, the Jinx took command at Monterrey, and the Chameleon was sent to Irapuato as Chief of Operations. In a word, they'd gained control of the entire northern half of the country and of the railroads.

To support Juan Valdivia's candidacy, two political parties were formed: the P.R.R.I. (Party for Restoration of Revolutionary Ideals) headed by Fatty Artajo, and the R.I.P. (Revolutionary Intellectuals' Party) led by that well-known writer, lawyer (and, incidentally, Major General) Giovanni Pittorelli. Despite his Italian-sounding name, he was a Mexican, born and bred.

That was the way things stood. I had no intention of getting involved in politics because the last few months had brought me enough headaches. But then I received a letter that made me change my mind. It read:

You are hereby ordered to report to Mexico City for a meeting of all Regional Commanders, to take place on [the date came here] for the purpose of coordinating plans for military operations during the forthcoming elections.

It was signed by Vidal Sánchez. Another trip to the capital! I started out once again, never realizing that this journey—like every other before it—would be another step in my headlong race toward catastrophe.

When the train pulled into the station, I was somewhat surprised to see Fatty Artajo and Germán Trenza waiting on the platform. At first I pretended not to see them, but when they opened their arms to me, I remembered that in the heart of any soldier, comradeship will always win out over the baser passions. We embraced eagerly in complete reconciliation.

Fatty sent his aide to the Cosmopolita Hotel with my baggage, and we got into Trenza's Packard and drove to a *cantina* "to talk things over," as they put it.

I should have known what to expect. Vieyra was an important area from a strategic military viewpoint, big enough to make them want me on their side. They asked me to join the P.R.R.I.

"But Juan Valdivia isn't popular!" I protested.

"That's precisely why he needs the army's support," they answered. That made sense.

There was only one other possible candidate: Gregorio Meléndez, an engineer.

"No engineer will ever win an election in Mexico," Trenza pointed out. "Remember what happened to Bonilla."

We all know what happened to Bonilla.

"Count me in," I told them.

We embraced to seal the bargain. It is not true that I was intoxicated at the time, as Artajo has insinuated in his *Memoirs*.

"The function of the armed forces is to see to it that the citizens' will is respected and to guarantee the people's freedom to express that will," Vidal Sánchez told us very solemnly at the meeting. (This was a complete about-face from what he'd said to me about "Where did you get the idea anyone gives a damn about a free election?" and all that.) "For this reason, as of this moment, all military personnel in command of troops are expressly forbidden to belong to any political party."

We were stunned into silence. All of us were seated at a long table, Vidal at the head. No one dared to speak up in front of thirty colleagues.

"This isn't an order," (it was always the same story: he'd say "expressly forbidden" and then "this isn't an order") "but merely a suggestion. Can I count on your cooperation?"

Needless to say, we all said yes. Then we went to Juan Valdivia's house to figure out a way to squirm out of our promise. It would be better for the party to lose the prestige of our membership than for us to lose our commands. We found a solution, and it was a simple one: Instead of Fatty Artajo, the President of the P.R.R.I. would be Horacio Flores, an eloquent if obscure Deputy, and we'd support him from behind the scenes. While it would appear that the party's sole assets were two remarkable orators (Horacio and Juan Valdivia), it would actually boast some twenty thousand fully armed and equipped troops. During our talk, Juan Valdivia promised to make me Secretary of Communications and Public Works. Fatty Artajo would get War and the Navy, and Germán Trenza would be the new Secretary of the Interior.

As soon as these important arrangements had been made, I went back to Vieyra, bursting with enthusiasm. We founded a local branch of the P.R.R.I. and, with the financial aid of a wealthy landowner who had his eye on the State governorship, we organized a gigantic rally to welcome our candidate on his campaign tour.

Upon his arrival at Vieyra on April 23, Valdivia made a stirring speech at the railroad station, promising his supporters enforcement of the Revolutionary principle of separation of Church and State (religious persecution) and agrarian reform. This cost us the backing of the said landowner, but the crowd was delighted. (We'd had a hard time getting the audience together and had to pay them two pesos a head.) We almost had a riot on our hands when Juan said, "There are still trails to be blazed, bridges to be burned!" The timely intervention of a rifle squad kept the mob under control.

"Juan, try to be a little less radical in your speeches," I told him during the banquet given in his honor by the Farmers' Union at the Vieyra Casino. And he listened to me because he knew I was giving him good advice. He made an after-dinner speech promising credits and guaranteed farm prices; he was given a standing ovation. Juan was the perfect candidate; he had a promise for everyone, for every occasion, and I never heard him repeat himself. Come to think of it, I never saw him keep any of his promises either.

A few days after the banquet, I received the following bulletin from the Ministry of War:

ALL COMMANDERS, OFFICERS, AND TROOPS OF THE NA-
TIONAL ARMY ARE HEREBY NOTIFIED THAT MAJOR GENERAL
MELITÓN ANGUIANO IS ASSUMING FULL CHARGE OF THIS
MINISTRY, IN SUBSTITUTION OF MAJOR GENERAL VIDAL SÁN-
CHEZ, WHO HAS RESIGNED FROM HIS POST IN ORDER TO EN-
GAGE IN POLITICAL ACTIVITIES.

This news came as a blow, not only because my job was
hanging by a thread again, not only because I'd have to resign (the customary procedure in these cases), but because
an opponent much more powerful than Meléndez was en-
tering the political arena against Valdivia.

I rushed to the Frances Hotel, Valdivia's headquarters
during his State-wide tour.

Juan was puzzled when I told him about the announcement.
"He can't run," he said. "It would be unconstitutional."

I didn't know what to do. Should I send in my resignation
or wait until it was requested?

"Wait and see what happens," was Juan's wise counsel.
"One of these days they might accept it, and what would
you do then?"

On the following day, Horacio Flores arrived on the noon
train with an astonishing message. Vidal Sánchez wanted to
talk to Juan and Horacio, candidate and President of the
P.R.R.I., respectively. Valdivia cut short his tour that was
barely getting under way, and they set off for Mexico City.

I still didn't know what to do about my resignation and
sent a telegram to Germán Trenza asking for his opinion. He
replied something like this:

DO NOT RESIGN STOP LET THEM FIRE US IF THEY DARE.

I took his advice because I suspected that he might be
right and that they wouldn't dare. They didn't.

Chapter VIII

One morning I was out shooting rabbits with Captain Benítez, my best marksman. We saw three men on horseback
coming in our direction. I recognized my aide, but didn't
know who the other two were. They were wearing civilian
clothing, but their Stetsons gave them away as army men.

Soon they came close enough for me to identify German
Trenza and Anastasio Rodríguez. They looked serious but
not too unhappy, so I had no way of knowing if they were
bringing good news or bad.

We moved away to talk under some trees, out of earshot
of Benítez and my aide.

"Vidal wants to form a Coalition Party," Trenza told me.
I didn't know what to make of this announcement because I
wasn't sure I understood exactly what it meant.

"What's that?" I asked.

They explained that Vidal Sánchez wanted to bring all
the Revolutionary factions and groups together into a single
political party. He'd already convinced the M.U.C., the
P.U.C., the F.U.C., the P.O.P., the M.F.R.U., the
C.R.P.T. and the S.P.Q.R., and now he wanted the support
of the P.R.R.I. and the R.I.P. I thought back to what Vidal
had told me about true Revolutionaries: "We're still in the
minority . . . we have to stick together . . ." Et cetera . . .
et cetera.

"What's in it for us?" I asked.

"The Presidency," Anastasio replied. "It looks as if the candidate of the Coalition Party will probably be Juan Valdivia."

"If the coalition nominates Juan, Meléndez has agreed to withdraw his candidacy," Trenza added.

Juan Valdivia was practically on the throne!

"We've got the election sewed up," Anastasio said.

"Oh, sure! But so do a couple of hundred others," I told them, and I was absolutely right. When the time came to hand out jobs there wouldn't be enough good ones to go around to reward such a big party.

"That's why we're here," Trenza said. "To get your opinion. There's no reason why we should go along with Vidal except on our own terms. We've got a good candidate, the campaign is running well, and we control more than half the army. All that puts us in a pretty good bargaining position."

We mounted the three horses, leaving the aide and Benítez to return on foot.

"What do I get?" I demanded.

"What do you want?"

"Communications, like we'd planned."

"Everybody wants Communications!" Trenza protested.

"Then we'll just have to get rid of some people," I replied.

"That's what I say," Trenza said. That was generous of him because his own job as Secretary of the Interior was in the bag.

Then I turned to Anastasio who, as I've mentioned before, was a very quiet person, and asked him:

"And what did you get?"

He took off his hat, scratched his head, then explained that they'd promised him that they'd do whatever they could to get him elected Mayor of his hometown. I was indignant.

"That's not fair! After years and years of sacrifice, all you get is a crummy one-horse town?" In the Revolution, Anastasio had won the Battle of Zapopan against enormous odds, and now they were about to shove him into the background just because he wasn't much of a talker.

"You've got to speak up for yourself," I told him, "and not just for your own sake; you're duty-bound to defend the honor of the army."

That was my honest opinion. He didn't answer.

We rode in silence for a while and, after some deep thought, I made up my mind:

"I don't like the idea of this Coalition Party one bit."

"Neither do I," Trenza agreed. "But it's too big to fight." There was no question about that.

The key to the problem was becoming very clear: If you find yourself in the vicinity of a steamroller, it's always a good idea to be on top of it and not underneath.

Trenza was apparently thinking along the same lines.

"There's only one thing we can do, Lupe," he said, "and that's to make very sure that we keep control of this Coalition Party in our own hands."

By this time we'd reached the Moorish-style home I'd had built in Vieyra. Matilde, paragon of Mexican womanhood, was standing at the gate waiting for us. The two men greeted her affectionately, and we went into my study.

"I want to be Secretary—" I reminded them as soon as we were seated, "—of anything, but a Secretary." I knew that the time had come to stand up and be counted. *Now or never!* I told myself.

Germán Trenza agreed with me that we had to be bold in making our demands. After a long discussion, we came up with the following ideas: First of all, we'd make Vidal Sánchez give us three Ministry posts, including Secretary of War and the Navy, six regional commanderships, and eight governorships. He could keep the Chamber of Deputies, the Diplomatic Corps, and all that other stuff he's so interested in, to give out to his puppets. If he accepted our terms, well and good. But if he didn't—that is, if he tried to haggle with us—we'd settle for less . . . "in principle." Then we'd carry out the following maneuver: We'd enlist the aid of a certain unscrupulous individual who, despite a complete lack of any civic—or even manly—virtue, had a reputation for being an untiring champion of every cause of the workingman. Secretly, we'd help him form a Workers' Party, whose candidate would be Peahead Hernández, the Father of Labor Politics himself! Naturally, the socialist groups (the M.F.R.U., C.R.P.T., and S.P.Q.R.) would pull out of the coalition and throw their support to the Workers' Party. All this would take a lot of people out of the running when President Juan Valdivia started repaying political favors with jobs. (It was perfectly obvious that Peahead Hernández didn't have the ghost of a chance to win the election; he was black-listed by the U.S. government because of his radical ideas.)

We telephoned Mexico City and reported our conversation to Juan Valdivia. He congratulated us and said he thought we'd come up with a foolproof plan.

"I'll go to see Vidal right now with our proposals," he said, and hung up.

We went to the casino and were just about to order lunch when the manager came to our table and said there was a long-distance call for me. All three of us jumped up and ran to the telephone.

It was Juan.

"I can't understand it," he said. "Vidal accepted all our conditions!"

We should have smelled a rat, it had been so easy, but we were so happy, we didn't suspect a thing. It never occurred to us that if we'd spent two hours thinking of a way to eliminate people, Vidal Sánchez had spent six months doing the very same thing.

Feeling the need for some wholesome relaxation from the day's tensions, we spent the night at Aurora Carrasco's establishment.

Chapter IX

There was a "secret pact" among the parties that were to be unified; their separate campaigns would be conducted as usual until July 25, the date when the coalition would be officially announced. Gregorio Meléndez would then withdraw his candidacy, accepting the post of Secretary of Finance in Juan Valdivia's Cabinet. This, as I have said, was the "secret pact."

Valdivia's campaign went ahead smoothly; it was so successful that we were almost sorry we'd even bothered to make any deals with all those wicked people who had no true Revolutionary spirit. In Sayula, an exuberant crowd unhooked our candidate's railcar and pushed it themselves for three kilometers (this display of enthusiasm cost the Party a small fortune); in Guateque, his speech on agrarian policy moved the demonstrators so deeply that they ended up lynching a local wealthy landowner; in Las Mangas there was some shooting, and the army had to be called in. In Monterrey, on the other hand, he made a speech at the Industrialists' Club that was so conservative and reactionary that Vidal Sánchez warned him to be more careful. In Tabasco he so inspired his audience that he caused the death of two individuals suspected (mistakenly) of being Catholic priests, while in Moroleón, where he gave a pro-Catholic speech, the victim was a Methodist minister. In summary, although there were ups and downs, the results were more than satisfactory.

Meléndez, the other candidate, inspired no enthusiasm anywhere, even though the Mexico City newspapers supported him (for a price, no doubt).

We decided we should "feel out the sympathies of the Ministry of War," as Fatty Artajo said. The three Regional Commanders (Artajo himself, Trenza, and I) would send in requisitions for three thousand extra cartridges per soldier "for some clean-up operations."

I was sure I wouldn't get the ammunition. For one thing, there was nothing to clean up in my sector. By some good fortune, I hadn't yet run into the Acting President, Eulalio Pérez, but I knew that if he found out about the request, he'd raise the roof. The five million cartridges were delivered very promptly. What a surprise! I couldn't believe it and suspected the ammunition might be defective, but Captain Benítez and I tested it, and it was fine. Not imported, domestic-made, but fine. It was a gesture of goodwill that should have made me suspicious because there was no need for it.

The months passed by without incident until July. Juan Valdivia decided to wind up his campaign with a grand banquet for all the political, social, financial, diplomatic, and military bigwigs of the country. It would be his last chance to give the Party a boost and tie up any loose ends before the coalition was announced.

This important event was to take place at Juan's mansion in Cuernavaca; he set the date: the fateful July 23, 1929.

"You all have to be there," he instructed us. "We have to show our strength."

So we all went, and consummated one of the most incredible blunders in the political history of Mexico.

* * *

The residence, constructed with funds of unknown origin, was of the purest Andalusian style. No one ever knew for sure how many rooms it contained, there were so many. It had a courtyard with a fountain (a copy of the Quixote Fountain in Mexico City's Chapultepec Park), a couple of gazebos, an enormous garden, a swimming pool, and a steambath that could accommodate seventy people.

My friends and I arrived the night before the dinner. We needed some time together to settle a few points of our program for the following day. I made the trip from Mexico City in the Packard Germán Trenza drove so expertly.

Preparations were in full swing when we arrived. A company of army engineers that Juan had borrowed from the local commandant was busily destroying the rose garden to make room for a stage (there was to be a performance of some folk dances). Inside the house we found riotous activity; ladders stood everywhere, furniture was being moved back and forth, servants scurried here and there with heavy baskets of food. Juan's wife, who was directing all this traffic from the huge entry hall, told us her husband was playing billiards. While our aides took our luggage upstairs to the rooms assigned to us, we went to the basement game room.

Juan was playing with Fatty Artajo, who was a rotten player. When we appeared, they put down their cues and looked solemn.

"We're going to have to ask you to make a great sacrifice, Lupe."

I didn't know what Fatty was driving at and asked him to explain.

"You tell him," Fatty pleaded with Valdivia, who replied, "No, you tell him," and they quibbled about it for a while.

"It's about you and Eulalio Pérez," Valdivia finally blurted out.

"Here we go again!" I said. I knew what he was leading up to. Valdivia gave a long list of reasons why "for the sake of the Party" we needed the Acting President's support. If we hoped to get it, he said, I'd have to make peace with Pérez.

"I'd sooner die than make up with that crook!" I said. I hadn't told anyone that the matter of the watch had been cleared up or that the watch was in my pocket at that very moment. I called him a crook because Eulalio Pérez *was* a crook.

"Do it for the sake of the Revolution," Fatty Artajo begged and then he added, almost prophetically, "We don't want any unpleasant surprises later on."

I turned to Germán Trenza for support, but he was on their side.

"I'd hate to see all our plans fall apart just because you're set on being selfish and stubborn."

They pointed out how well everything was going and reminded me of the rosy future awaiting all of us, et cetera, et cetera. They were so insistent I finally had to give in.

"Go to his house and straighten things out with him," Artajo urged. Pérez owned a weekend home in Cuernavaca. "He should be in town by noon."

Then I said yes, fine, okay, I'd patch things up with Eulalio, but how was I going to go about it? What could I say to him?

We wrestled with the problem until two in the morning. By that time the Chameleon, Anastasio, and the Jinx had arrived. The Chameleon was an expert on apologies.

"Play dumb. Tell him you thought he was somebody else, somebody you have a quarrel with, and that later you found out that that somebody had left the cemetery with the rest of us, that you remembered what the voice sounded like and suddenly realized that it must have been Eulalio you pushed, and that you're terribly sorry, you're absolutely mortified, and all that.''

This didn't sound half bad to me; I'd save face, and so would Pérez. I assured them that within twelve hours I'd have made peace with the Acting President.

Then we talked about what each of us was going to say and do the following day. Our political program consisted of a campaign of smears against the socialist parties. The plan that Germán, Anastasio, and I had worked out to secretly organize another party and nominate Peahead Hernández was approved unanimously by the others. We were still at it at daybreak.

I lay down to rest awhile, but I couldn't sleep because just when my eyes were closing, the army engineers arrived again and started making a racket.

I got up at nine. I took a bath, put on a nifty Palm Beach suit, stuck the Smith and Wesson under my arm, and went down for breakfast.

By that time the rose garden was completely demolished and the stage was in place; the smoke of fifteen barbecue pits flooded the house, making the air unbreathable. I went to the kitchen where Valdivia's wife, Clarita, and a dozen servants were busy preparing *mole poblano* for 250 guests. The fumes of the required seven different kinds of chilies mixed with the barbecue smoke and gave me a coughing fit. When I recovered, Clarita, always the perfect hostess, said good morning and led me to a table where the Chameleon was eating pork rinds cooked in green sauce, while his aide polished his boots. Clarita removed a suckling pig from a chair and invited me to sit down. I asked her if I could have a cup of hot chocolate.

''Don't you think it's strange that Pittorelli hasn't come to

Cuernavaca yet?'' the Chameleon asked. We were supposed
to meet with that gentleman to work out some joint plans.
(He was the head of the R.I.P., the other party supporting
Valdivia.)

"He told me he was planning to come a day ahead of time
and spend the night at the Vistahermosa Hotel.''

This was another danger signal that should have put us on
alert!

After breakfast we went for a walk through the garden,
where we came upon Valdivia rehearsing his speech.

"The moment has come for the Nation . . .'' he was saying, lifting his hand in a graceful gesture. We left him to his
rhetoric.

We found Anastasio in a bathing suit at the pool, the only
athlete in our group, and Horacio Flores, the orator, who
had just arrived from Mexico City.

"There are troops on the highway,'' he told us.

Like a shooting star, the image of the unfortunate General
Serrano flashed into my mind's eye. Just two years earlier
he had been shot on this same highway, at precisely the time
when he felt most certain he would become the next President of the Republic.

"Of course there are,'' said the Jinx, joining us. "A lot of
important people will be at the banquet. The troops are there
for security.''

"What companies were they from?'' asked the Chameleon, unconvinced by this reasoning.

Unfortunately, Horacio wasn't a soldier and didn't know
what we were talking about.

"What were the numbers? You know, the little numbers
here on the collar,'' we explained to him. It was no use; he
hadn't noticed.

We put it out of our minds and changed the subject. At the

stroke of eleven, I put on my Stetson, took my leave, and went to carry out my unpleasant mission.

Juan lent me his Studebaker. I had a hard time driving it because I was unfamiliar with both the area and the automobile, but at last I reached Pérez's estate. The house was enormous and it was surrounded by a stone wall. I stopped the automobile at the gate, got out, and knocked. I heard shouts for the "corporal of the guard" from within and, when the gatehouse window opened, I saw an enlisted man who had served under me for many years. We exchanged friendly greetings, then I asked for Pérez.

"The President isn't here—neither is anybody else. The house is completely empty for the first time all year."

Then I knew that something was going on. I said goodbye hurriedly, got into the Studebaker, and sped back to Juan's house as if the devil himself were at my heels.

The army engineers were gone.

"We've walked right into a trap, boys," I announced, "like the one they set for Serrano."

Of course, they were all alarmed. The Chameleon said:

"If they're planning to [I cannot repeat the word] us, they'd never do it in front of the Diplomatic Corps. Let's try to call Jefferson or the French ambassador. If they're in town, we have nothing to worry about."

Juan Valdivia picked up the receiver, and a look of terror spread across his face.

"The lines have been cut!" he told us.

Those miserable engineers must have done it.

"Now all we need is for them to send a detachment to 'protect' us," Trenza said. A detachment was sent for Serrano's protection; they never left his side until he was executed.

Then I spoke:

"We have to break the siege and get away now before it's too late." This is exactly what I said, and not, "Let's get all our troops together and shoot it out,'' as Fatty Artajo has claimed in his *Memoirs*. But even if I had said that, I wouldn't be ashamed to admit it and, anyway, things wouldn't have turned out any differently.

Chapter X

The discovery of the cut telephone lines convinced us. There was no longer the slightest doubt that we were in a trap and that if we wanted to get out of it alive, we had to break the siege, as I'd already mentioned so opportunely. So nothing of what Fatty Artajo wrote ("Lupe Arroyo was frightened") is true. We were all scared and so was he. He was the one who suggested we disguise ourselves; he even put on a straw hat and would have gotten into the gardener's overalls if he'd been able to squeeze into them.

"Send somebody for the automobiles," Valdivia ordered.

"Tell them to make sure the gasoline tanks are full," added Trenza.

"To arms!" I shouted.

Fortunately, the Chameleon kept his head. If he hadn't, I don't know how this episode would have turned out.

"What do you expect to do," he asked, "shoot your way into Mexíco City?" He was right. It wasn't as simple as that. "If, as we've been told, there are troops on the highway, you can be damned sure they're not there to salute us as we ride by."

Right again! All our haste would lead nowhere but straight into the lion's mouth. People I've told this story to invariably ask why we were so frightened. They don't realize that anyone who gets involved in politics has to be prepared for the worst. What happened later illustrates that our alarm was perfectly justified.

But, as I was saying, the Chameleon's words made us abandon our plans to return to Mexico City by highway.

The Jinx, who had no common sense at all, suggested that we drive south to Acapulco, take a ship from there to Manzanillo, and then travel back to our command posts by train. This journey would take at least a week.

"Why go to our command posts at all? Let's head for the border," Valdivia said. This statement should have given us an inkling of the magnitude of his cowardice. But nobody took his idea seriously, so we simply explained to him that things weren't so bleak that we had to drop everything and run to the border like scared rabbits.

"The people need you, General," said Horacio Flores, the demagogue of the group. Valdivia was persuaded.

Someone suggested we ought to travel at night.

"If we wait for dark," I said, "we may be cold by then— stiff too!"

And the quibbling continued. Each of us proposed a plan of escape, the others discussed its pros and cons and finally decided if the idea was good or bad. We were still arguing at one o'clock.

"Juan, the *mariachi* band is here," announced Clarita, poking her head in at the door.

Valdivia astonished her with a curse because he was in no mood to worry about details like that.

"Tell them to play, ma'am," the Chameleon advised. "The louder, the better."

The opening strains of "Dios Nunca Muere" (God Never Dies) reminded us that death was stalking us, and we decided to get moving. The back gate opened onto an alley, so we had three automobiles parked there. Our aides were loading our luggage when the telephone rang. We looked at one another silently. Valdivia answered. It was Central calling to report that the lines had been repaired.

Our fear melted just as quickly as it had been aroused two hours earlier. And then suddenly everybody was blaming me.

"You almost ruined my political career!" I was told by the gentleman who was ready to flee to the border a short while earlier.

I argued that the repair of the telephone lines didn't explain why there were troops on the highway, why Pérez hadn't arrived, where Pittorelli was. They jeered.

The least fashionable of those invited to the banquet started to arrive: the leader of the Chamber of Deputies, Peahead Hernández (Champion of the Workers), a man who had made a fortune selling liquor on the border, and the individual who had organized the first tenants' strike in Mexico City; some ladies also made an appearance.

Juan Valdivia changed into a *charro* suit with gold piping and went out to greet his guests.

When Jefferson arrived, Fatty Artajo threw me a scathing glance, as if to say I was responsible for starting a totally uncalled-for panic. The *mariachi* band interrupted the song they had been playing, and "The Star-Spangled Banner" surged majestically from the Artillery Band.

"You and your jitters," snarled Fatty, who'd been more scared than any of the rest of us a short half-hour earlier.

"Let's just wait and see if Pérez shows up," I answered. I prayed to God he wouldn't, partly because I was in no hurry to see him, but mostly because I didn't want my friends to make fun of me.

Juan Valdivia thought it would be in poor taste to serve alcoholic beverages in the presence of the representative of a country under Prohibition, so he ordered the waiters to put out of sight the seventy-two cases of aperitifs, cordials, sparkling wines, scotch, gin, and rum that had been provided for the guests' consumption. This action provoked a feeling of hostility toward the United States. The party began to drag.

It was still dragging when an acquaintance approached me and gave me this news:

"Pittorelli's been arrested."

"What for?" I asked.

"For writing General González's 'Political Testament.' "

My heart sank as it dawned on me that I was hearing the announcement of Valdivia's political downfall . . . and my own. This explained the troops on the highway. I rushed away to tell the others.

We gathered in the game room and the arguments started all over: Do we go? Do we stay? Why should we go? What about the troops on the road? At least Valdivia didn't bring up the idea of going to the border this time. Our decision to declare an open insurrection was a unanimous one; it wasn't my idea alone, as Artajo has written.

"We'd better get started before they arrest us," Trenza urged with wisdom.

The Chameleon suggested we take the Cuautla road instead of the main highway, and we agreed. If there were any surprises waiting for us in Mexico City, they'd be on the principal road.

We left the game room and immediately noticed that Jefferson had vanished, as if by magic. This fueled our fears and hastened our departure.

"Bring out the liquor," Valdivia commanded.

And while drinks were being served and the party began to liven up again, we slipped out inconspicuously, got into the automobiles, and headed toward the Cuautla road.

It was a ghastly trip because the road was full of potholes, but we didn't come across a single soldier until we reached Yautepec, and the one we saw there was walking some horses and just watched us ride by.

We got to Mexico City at midnight and went to Trenza's house. We entered very quietly, expecting to find the police waiting for us, but we found nobody but Camila and the maid, both sound asleep.

We went our separate ways after solemnly swearing that we would strictly follow the "emergency plan" we'd prepared in April. The next day I rode back to Vieyra in the mail car of the express. Fortunately, the guard was a fellow I knew; he'd helped us during the political campaign.

Our pictures were plastered across the front pages of the papers that day, accompanied by a completely inaccurate article that read: "GENERALS' CONSPIRACY DISCOVERED. GENERALS [our names were listed here] PLOTTED TO OVERTHROW THE GOVERNMENT. THE TRAITORS WERE TAKEN PRISONER IN CUERNAVACA BY FEDERAL FORCES. PEACE AND TRANQUILLITY HAVE BEEN RESTORED IN THE ENTIRE NATION," and it went on for two whole pages saying that everything was peaceful and that we were scoundrels.

As I read this article, comfortably propped against some mailbags, it occurred to me that our timely departure had frustrated one of the most diabolical schemes ever conceived in Mexican politics . . . murky enough until then.

Pittorelli "confessed" he was the author of González's "Political Testament," which was perfectly true, but he also said that we'd paid him to write it, and that was an out-and-out lie! We didn't expose him, because that wouldn't have been to our advantage, but we never told him to write it either. And the confession just happened to be made only two days before the unification of the parties and the announcement of the coalition candidate; it happened to be serious enough not only to ruin a candidate, but to put at least half a dozen people behind bars; and they all just happened to be together that day at Juan Valdivia's banquet. All these coincidences and, to top it all off, the three thousand cartridges per soldier they'd just sent us, were products of the warped mind of Vidal Sánchez, who must have been knocking his head against the wall in a fury because we'd managed to slip between his claws.

Chapter XI

The Ministry of War sent Cenón Hurtado telegraphic instructions to take command at Vieyra and to arrest me if I showed up there, but when I walked into my office and found him comfortably installed at my desk, he scrambled to his feet and saluted.

As soon as I made sure that the situation was under control (*my* control), I sent Matilde and the children to visit her brother, a customs inspector at Ciudad Juárez. This was not an act of defeatism, but one of precaution, because everyone knows that the relatives of Revolutionaries have very seldom suffered reprisals. However, I didn't want it to be said sometime in the future, "there was an exception in the case of General José Guadalupe Arroyo." And so, as I've already said, I sent Matilde and the kids to Ciudad Juárez, just across the border from El Paso, Texas. Then I called a meeting of the company commanders.

When they arrived, I told them:

"The first thing we have to do is gain, then keep, control of all railroads, telegraph lines, and banks." Then I said that Pérez's administration was a violation of the Constitution and all that, and ended with, "Any of you who are unwilling to join forces with us may retire with full military honors." No one moved from his seat.

Then I briefed them on my campaign strategy which, as I have mentioned earlier, was based on the one my colleagues and I had prepared way back in April. My mission was to take Apapátaro, capital of the State of the same name, and then, if I could, Cuévano, the important rail center where we would all meet: Fatty Artajo would come from Sonora, Germán Trenza from Tamaulipas, the Jinx from Monterrey, and the Chameleon from Irapuato. Valdivia, Anastasio, and Horacio Flores were in Tamaulipas with Trenza. Once we joined forces in Cuévano, we would march on the Nation's capital, form an interim government, call new elections, et cetera, et cetera, et cetera.

After consultation with my commanders (and not by my-self, with my "customary despotism" as Cenón Hurtado testified during the court-martial held later), I decided to arrest the Governor, Virgilio Urquiza, the owner of the Vieyra Bank, and four of the most powerful members of the Farm-ers' Union, and to demand a ransom of 600,000 pesos. If that quantity wasn't delivered within twenty-four hours, they would be executed.

I would like to add an explanation here and justify this ac-tion that brought so much criticism: Uppermost in our thoughts was the country's welfare; the Nation was in the hands of a heartless murderer, Vidal Sánchez, and of a com-mon criminal, Eulalio Pérez; the Nation had to be liberated. She could be freed only by an army and we all know that an army on the march is something that costs a lot of money. Now, then, Mexico's lower classes are very generous with their blood whenever a just cause is at stake. But no army has ever been run on public monetary donations. The neces-sary funds can be gotten from only one of two places: the strongboxes of the wealthy or the government of the United States. Since we couldn't hope for the support—or even the sympathy—of the latter, we had to set our sights on the former.

Has any rich Mexican ever given any money voluntarily

for any cause? Patriotic or otherwise? Never! That's why we threw these six celebrities into the post guardhouse.

The banker's wife, dissolved in tears, came to plead with me not to shoot her husband.

"Nobody's going to shoot him, ma'am," I said, trying to calm her down. "He'll be released just as soon as I get the ransom money."

"My husband may own a bank, but we're really very poor," she wailed. Her brazenness made me want to execute *her*.

Seeing that I was dealing with a woman with good business sense, I gave her the usual speech: "I'll give you a voucher and as soon as the Revolution triumphs, the new government will repay your investment with interest compounded at four percent per annum." She didn't believe a word of it because, unfortunately, many have made the same promises and never kept them.

She lifted her veil (because she was wearing a hat and everything) and I felt instinctively that she loved her husband so dearly that she would be receptive to my advances if I agreed to let him go. Or rather, she loved his money so dearly. I stood there, looking her over, then thought to myself: *This woman isn't worth anywhere near 600,000 pesos,* but said nothing to her.

When she realized that her attempt at seduction would get her nowhere, she decided to lay her cards on the table.

"Listen, General, I can tell you're a reasonable man. Look at it this way: If you put six people in jail and demand one ransom for the lot, their families are going to expect the one who seems to be the richest—my husband—to pay for all of them. Why don't you ask for one hundred thousand pesos apiece and say you'll shoot the ones who don't pay? You'll have your money tomorrow. You'll see."

I was amazed that a woman could be so shrewd in money

matters. I gave orders to notify the families of the new conditions. The second part of her strategy was also profitable. Since nobody had that much cash, they had to go to her and her bank to sell their lands, houses, stocks, and bonds—at her prices.

Since we'd chosen carefully and had picked six really rich hostages, by the next day we had the ransom money for all of them except the Governor, whose only capital was the State Treasury, and we'd beaten him to it and had already emptied it out. I spared his life and we released all six.

When they were about to leave my office, I told them:

"This money you have given us is not lost. We are holding it for you in trust. When the Revolution triumphs . . ." Et cetera.

They went away unconvinced. They were right not to believe me because they never saw their money again.

Encouraged by our success, my company commanders and I decided to arrest fifteen more ranchers the following day, but when my men went out to look for them, we discovered that all the rich men of the city had gone into hiding—God alone knew where. They couldn't have gotten very far because we'd captured the two trains that had come through in those days, but since we couldn't spare the time to search for them, we decided to take Father Jorge, who was still plying his priestly trade in the Guadalupe Sanctuary in violation of all the anti-Church laws. We put him in the guardhouse and planned to set his ransom at fifty thousand pesos. But no sooner had the cell door closed behind him when a crowd of sanctimonious knee-benders appeared, protesting what they called "arbitrary discrimination."

Reluctant to make enemies of the masses, I ordered a mock cavalry charge to disperse the mob. I had Father Jorge released and his sacristan shot (just to show we weren't pushovers). My orders were carried out to the letter.

That was the last attempt I made to collect funds for the Revolution in Vieyra, because the next morning I marched out with all my men toward Apapátaro, Apapátaro.

Chapter XII

While these financial transactions were taking place, Captain Benítez, who was my chief technician and a very ingenious man, was busy improvising an armored car from an old American Smelting Company flatcar, the remains of a discarded tank car, our sole artillery piece (a 75mm. cannon for which we had exactly forty-two shells) and two Hotchkiss machine guns. This monstrosity was hitched in front of the engine like a battering ram and became our spearhead.

The infantry was transported in the two trains we had captured, while the cavalry troops rode their mounts to Apapátaro, some 150 kilometers away. My plan was for the infantry to take the city by surprise. If this first effort was unsuccessful, we would retreat a little, wait for the cavalry to arrive, and launch a second, full-force attack.

The city of Vieyra had no strategic value, so we evacuated it, taking no more than we needed. I knew that time was of the essence because our entire future depended on occupying Apapátaro.

We traveled by night in three trains, each staying one kilometer behind the one ahead of it. The first was made up of the armored car described above, the locomotive, and a flatcar carrying a company of infantry. The Twelfth Battalion, under the command of Cenón Hurtado, followed in the second train, and the rest of the troops brought up the rear in the third train. Needless to say, I traveled in the first train with Captain Benítez.

Just outside Los Lobos the tracks had been destroyed; we almost derailed. Fortunately, we had come well prepared. We had a full supply of repair equipment in the last train and, after a two-hour delay, we were rolling again.

I gave orders for all lights to be turned off—even the headlight on the lead engine—because I didn't want anyone to be able to calculate our strength.

Somebody started shooting at us about ten kilometers outside Apapátaro, but we returned the gunfire with such a din that they were quickly silenced. We went on our way once more.

By the time Apapátaro appeared on the horizon, the sun was coming up.

"So much the better," I said. "Let them see we're not coming empty-handed."

I called a halt some two hundred meters from the station. The other trains stopped farther back.

"Let them have a taste of the cannon," I told Benítez. "Let's see what they think of that!"

"Where should I aim, General?"

I pointed to the cathedral towers, the most visible target in the early-morning light, and he fired the shell that would go down in history. It landed on the steps of the State Legislature.

After three more cannon blasts, we pulled into the station. A spray from our two Hotchkisses shattered all the windows. Nobody shot back at us. The infantry company occupied the station without meeting any resistance; as a matter of fact, they didn't meet anyone.

Leaving a detachment to guard the station, we moved back to a good vantage point to resume our shelling. Meanwhile, the rest of the infantry got off the train and took combat positions.

Benítez fired the cannon again, and this time he did hit one of the cathedral towers.

Just then a captain carrying a white flag appeared; he had a message from the Apapátaro commander.

"General Chávez says he's on your side."

I didn't believe him. Why should General Chávez be on our side? Later, when we met at the station and he put himself and all his troops at our disposal, I learned that Chávez was on our side because he was scared.

"I don't want the civilian population inconvenienced," he told me during our talk.

"We'll disturb them as little as possible," I replied, "but bear in mind that we're practically empty-handed, and we have to find some money somewhere so we can keep moving." I made this statement in the presence of two witnesses: Captain Benítez and Cenón Hurtado.

We marched into the city triumphantly. That night we were the guests of honor at a ball, and the next day we threw fifty rich men into jail, including the Governor, the Mayor, and two prominent members of the State Legislature.

Chapter XIII

Criticism was heaped on me later because I didn't release these hostages although the ransom was paid. I'd like to set the record straight in these pages: The ransom was demanded to keep them from being shot, not to free them. And I didn't shoot anyone. It should be remembered that I was engaged in a full-scale war, in hostile territory, and that the carrying out of my military objectives left me no time to play games with the civilian population, and I had to keep the hostages in case anyone tried any dirty tricks. Besides, these people I'd jailed in Apapátaro were wealthy Mexicans, a vile breed; we should have done away with all of them just as soon as we won our independence from Spain! So I can't understand what anybody has to complain about; they accuse me of cruelty just because I kept a few bloodsuckers in jail for a couple of days.

Two days later, on August 3, Colonel Odilón Rendón came over to our side and brought his whole cavalry with him. I decided to review my troops. With the addition of the Apapátaro force of a full battalion and two cavalry squadrons, they now numbered over twenty-five hundred men. They were such a splendid sight that many of the city's inhabitants—especially the poorest ones, who are the most generous—came to volunteer. We organized them into two reserve companies, but I didn't intend to use them unless we could get some guns for them.

73

I decided to set up my base of operations in Apapátaro, and we conducted some clean-up operations in the surrounding areas; we also confiscated all the corn in the granaries and as many cattle as we could find. All this took us three days, and we were still at it when one of the *Cristero* leaders brought his men down out of the hills; he wanted to join forces with us because we were "all in the same struggle against oppression." Some of my officers advised me to arrest him, but I chose to play fair and accepted his services; I sent him to "spread the revolution," and for the next six years he kept the Regional Commander of the State of Guatáparo hopping.

By August 7 preparations were complete; we were scheduled to march on Cuévano the next day. At ten that morning, an Air Force Curtiss appeared; it circled the town several times and just when we expected it to start dropping bombs on us, it landed in a nearby field.

I leaped onto my horse and took a cavalry detachment to find out what was going on.

When I reached the field, I saw the airplane surrounded by a crowd of children and dogs; Anastasio Rodríguez and Juan Paredes, the famous aviator, emerged from the machine. We embraced with real pleasure and, leaving a squad to guard the aircraft, we went to my headquarters, which I had set up at the city's best hotel.

Anastasio brought news—some good, some bad, but all difficult to get out of him because he was such a clam and didn't like to talk.

"What news have you had about the Jinx?" I asked.

The Jinx had been unlucky, as usual. He'd been unable to complete his assignment (to take Laredo) and was waiting for somebody to send reinforcements. That meant that in the whole eastern half of the country we didn't hold a single point on the American border; and everybody knows that

Mexican revolutions are won by the side that controls the border.

"The newspapers said that Fatty Artajo occupied Culiacán," Anastasio told me, "but we haven't heard from him directly, so we have no way of knowing if it's true or just rumors."

Germán Trenza had made good progress and was getting into position to attack Cuévano. He was practically there. He'd sent me the Curtiss so I could use it for reconnaissance (he must have forgotten that the first place we'd find any fuel for it would be in Cuévano itself) and he'd sent Anastasio to help me. There was no news about the Chameleon.

"How did you know you'd find me here in Apapátaro?"

"It was in the papers."

A fine thing! The only way each of us could find out what the others were doing, in our own campaign, was through the corrupt Mexico City press!

Then he gave me a piece of news that made my skin crawl.

"They say a column is on the way from Mexico City to fight us. Macedonio Gálvez is the commander."

"Birds of a feather . . ." I muttered. And the thought crossed my mind that we were dealing with a gang of thieves. I swore then and there that one day Gálvez would pay for having stolen my pearl-handled pistol!

Later that day we held a staff meeting in the hotel's billiard room. Juan Paredes, who had flown over Cuévano, explained how the city's defenses were deployed.

The railroad tracks into Cuévano had been blown up both on our line and in the east, on Trenza's route. Heavy artillery was set up in the San Mateo hills. That would cause us some problems. We didn't know how many troops they had, but the commander used to be a friend of mine, and I knew he was no dope.

"Germán says that if you take out the artillery, he can take care of the rest," Anastasio said.

"For all we know, they could have a full division, and there's no way we can be sure," I said.

"I don't think we can handle that big a job. We don't have enough manpower and we're short on supplies," added Cenón Hurtado, who was a coward. No sooner were the words out of his mouth than I made up my mind to leave him behind at the Apapátaro garrison and launch the attack.

"We move out tonight," I announced, putting an end to the meeting.

Juan Paredes made another reconnaissance flight that was to be the last because the landing gear fell apart when he got back. We put the airplane up on one of the platforms we'd found and started our march at eight that night, with all our troops except one battalion and the volunteers; they were left behind with Cenón Hurtado.

Anastasio led the cavalry; it wasn't long before they caught up with our trains because we had to stop to repair the tracks. They rode on ahead of us. As soon as the rail line was fixed, we were under way again. At four in the morning, we heard some gunfire; our cavalry must be engaged in battle with the enemy's advance guards!

When Benítez began shelling the federal troops, they took to their heels in retreat. But we intercepted them in a pincer movement and took two hundred prisoners.

My men were exuberant, heartened by all these victories!

When we were ten kilometers from Cuévano, I ordered the troops off the train and, leading the infantry, set off to capture the hills of San Mateo. I sent Benítez ahead with the cannon; his shelling would serve as a diversionary strategy.

It was the following evening and everything was quiet.

Then Benítez started his bombardment. I ordered my men into combat formation and we advanced.

Instead of the fierce counterattack we were expecting, we came upon an enemy battalion in the process of moving to new positions facing our cannon fire; they almost trampled us in the dark.

We made quick work of them.

I ordered a charge up the hill. And there we went: I was in the lead and my men followed, yelling furiously. Luckily, the machine-gun nests were on the other side of the hill, awaiting Germán Trenza's attack from that direction, and we reached them before they had a chance to turn to face us; we swooped down on them and took them prisoners. Then we advanced to the top of the hill where the enemy artillery was emplaced, leaving part of our force to protect our rear.

We were moving very cautiously, fully expecting all hell to break loose at any moment, and suddenly we heard a dreadful clatter: the enemy's mules were running downhill, dragging the guns. They practically ran over us in their panic, trying to keep a few steps ahead of the heavy weapons. This incident scared us more than anything else in the whole battle, and we were on the verge of stampeding too. But after a while we calmed down and managed to capture the four guns, all the mules, the bags, baggage, ammunition, and everything else they were carrying.

When everything was quiet again in my sector, I sent word to Benítez to stop shelling us and, for the first time, I heard terrible shooting on the east side of Cuévano. I sent two companies out on reconnaissance.

As soon as the scouts left, Benítez came galloping in on a mule.

"I wasn't shelling you! I ran out of ammunition half an hour ago," he informed me.

Then I realized that the shrapnel falling all around us was

coming from the cannons of my dear friend Germán Trenza. Fortunately, his gun crew's marksmanship was so poor, they didn't cause much damage.

I immediately sent a messenger to report our position to Germán.

"Set up the cannons, Benítez, and aim at the city," I ordered.

"Yes, sir."

The bombardment began; it caused twenty casualties among the civilian population.

The rifle fire in the east came to an abrupt stop. When my reconnaissance group returned, we learned that the battle had been between two units of the troops defending the city. Stumbling around in the dark, each unit thought the other was the enemy (that is, us). This is one of the possible hazards of nighttime fighting.

"Cease fire!" I ordered when Trenza stopped shooting. We decided to postpone the attack until dawn because there'd already been enough confusion for one night.

At daybreak, we saw three long trains taking the retreating enemy toward Mexico City. We let out yells of joy because we had won the battle. Cuévano was ours! Two hours after the events I am relating here, the trains were intercepted by the Chameleon, who was moving his troops in from Irapuato very quietly.

The Cuévano commander managed to escape, and two days later he reported to Macedonio Gálvez at his headquarters in Celaya. By order of Vidal Sánchez, he was tried in court-martial on charges of high treason and executed. This was yet another of Vidal Sánchez's innumerable crimes, because the man was no traitor. We beat him because we fought with great courage and we were very lucky, that's all.

Chapter XIV

Germán Trenza had set up headquarters in a house near the station. As I approached, I saw some of his soldiers celebrating our victory; they were half-drunk although it was still early—not even nine in the morning. I dismounted and, turning my horse over to an aide, went into the house where Trenza was having breakfast with Camila, who never left his side. When he saw me, he rose and said:

"Lupe, we've won a great victory!"

" 'We' is a lot of people," I replied, and then complained about how badly the battle had been organized because, in the final analysis, Trenza's only contribution had been to shell me. He never engaged the enemy and, if the enemy hadn't decided to pull out of their own free will, the battle wouldn't have been half as glorious as it was.

But he was in no mood to worry about "unimportant little accidents," his term for the lack of coordination.

"If we won without being organized, imagine what will happen when we are!" He offered me a seat and Camila gave me some food. I accepted gratefully because it had been a long time since I'd had anything to eat.

There was good reason for our contentment. We were masters of a great rail center, the "gateway to the Central Plateau" as it's called in the geography books, a city with a population of 100,000—and we were only 700 kilometers from Mexico City.

We were still seated at the table when a delegation sent by the Cuévano City Council arrived.

"What kind of guarantees do you offer our citizens?" the President of the Chamber of Commerce inquired.

"None." We explained the Laws of War. Since the garrison had withdrawn, the city was at our mercy.

When the Chameleon arrived, we finalized plans and brought our troops into the city from three different directions. There was some looting, and by eight that night, six people had been executed for various crimes. The firing squad was a big help in reestablishing order, and the city was declared to be under martial law.

The following day, Trenza, as chief of the occupation, issued a decree confiscating all foodstuffs found in the city and all valuables found in the banks; he also took twenty hostages from among the best families—they might come in handy.

That afternoon, Valdivia and Horacio Flores arrived, bringing two more Air Force Curtisses and stacks of proclamations and political manifestos they'd had printed in Tampico. These were plastered on billboards and signposts, but no one ever read them; the people were scared and stayed indoors.

When the cavalry came in, Anastasio Rodríguez and Odilón Rendón joined us, and we held a commanders' meeting to decide the future of the Revolution.

"We need a Supreme Command," said Valdivia at the beginning of the meeting, and he talked for at least a quarter of an hour, at the end of which time we named him Commander in Chief of the East Army of the Restoration Forces (this was the name we'd picked for our movement). No sooner had he been invested in this important post than he stood up and told us:

"I don't think we ought to take another step until we have a gateway to the border."

We all disagreed. I insisted that we ought to attack Macedonio Gálvez quickly, before he had a chance to organize his column, and Germán Trenza supported my idea.

"We don't have enough manpower to try anything like that," said Chávez, who was always very cautious.

"I'm not so sure about that because we don't know how many men Macedonio is bringing with him," Trenza interrupted. "The only way to find out is to attack; if he beats us, we'll know we didn't have enough strength; if we win, we did."

I thought Trenza was right.

"Nothing ventured, nothing gained," I recited. "Besides, whatever his force may be now, the longer we wait, the worse it will be."

"I'd rather not make another move without Fatty Artajo's men," insisted Valdivia, our Commander in Chief. It was becoming obvious that what he really wanted was to stay put, right there in Cuévano.

The Chameleon suggested advancing along the Guadalajara railroad tracks, where we'd meet Fatty coming in from the north with his seven thousand men and four artillery regiments. We were all in favor of this plan and, then and there, we appointed the Chameleon Commander of the West Expeditionary Forces. They wouldn't listen to Germán and me; we still urged the attack on Gálvez. That action was postponed "for a more propitious occasion," as it read in the minutes of that meeting.

Valdivia, who was as stubborn as a mule, chimed in with the same old story: "We have to open a gateway to the border so we can have access to the American supply market."

He was forgetting that we had no money and couldn't buy anything.

"Let the Jinx open it," Trenza suggested.

"The Jinx can't open anything," the Chameleon replied. "He's the Jinx of the Mexican Army." He was absolutely right about that and we all knew it.

"I propose that Germán Trenza and Lupe Arroyo make a quick trip north, with hand-picked troops, and take the border town of Pacotas," Valdivia said.

It was at that moment that Trenza and I made our biggest mistake because we accepted the mission. We thought it would be a very simple matter to go north, occupy Pacotas, return to Cuévano, and then, with Fatty Artajo and his seven thousand men and four artillery regiments incorporated in our ranks, march against Macedonio Gálvez, who would be sitting in Celaya, twiddling his thumbs, patiently waiting for us to get good and ready to come and cut him to ribbons.

Chapter XV

The days that followed were filled with feverish activity. Despite torrential rains, Benítez worked miracles. He built an armored train that was a true masterpiece of military engineering. We were all so pleased with his work that Valdivia promoted him to Lieutenant Colonel.

On August 14, we started off, heading northward in three trains (the armored one and two transports). We took with us the Forty-fifth Regiment, two infantry battalions, and two 75mm. cannons.

The journey was completed without incident and we set up our lines fifteen kilometers outside Pacotas. There we were joined by the Jinx and his troops; they were a crestfallen lot because of the Laredo fiasco.

We were in the train (General Headquarters of the North Expeditionary Forces), planning our strategy, when we were notified that Mr. Robertson, the American consul in Pacotas, had just driven up in a flag-bedecked automobile and that he wanted to talk to us.

"If a single bullet falls on the other side of the river," warned Mr. Robertson, who was so red in the face we thought he was about to explode, "the Government of the United States will declare war on Mexico."

Our plan of attack included preliminary bombing to be

carried out in such a way that not *one* shell would drop on American territory—it would be more like a thousand.

"But surely you understand," Trenza argued very reasonably, "that if we're aiming from here to there, a few shells might easily overshoot the target and land on your side of the river."

Instead of replying, the consul whipped out a letter from his State Department which, according to one of our captains who understood English, said that they would indeed declare war on us if a single bullet went astray.

"Your country has always been very selfish!" I exclaimed. I was really burned up.

"We're sick and tired of all your revolutions," he shouted.

I said that this was no way to treat a country that had struggled as hard as Mexico had for Social Justice.

"We think it's very nice that you're struggling for Social Justice, but if you can't keep your revolution on your own side of the river, we'll come in and occupy Pacotas ourselves!"

Those were Mr. Robertson's very words.

Trenza wasn't his usual belligerent self that day. He said, quite pleasantly, "Surely you realize that we're trying to open up the border so we can do business with you."

"Well, then, open up the border and do business with us," the cunning *americano* replied, "but . . ." and he repeated his warning that if a single bullet went astray the United States would declare war on us. Et cetera.

Then he took out a sheet of paper he wanted us to sign. It was a formal commitment to respect the property of American citizens, and all that.

"I'm not signing anything!" I grumbled. I'd sooner have sent Mr. Robertson before a firing squad.

"If you refuse to sign," he answered, "the Armed Forces

of the United States of America will march in and occupy Pacotas tomorrow.''

Germán Trenza signed; the Jinx signed; I had no choice—I signed too.

''What do we do now?'' I asked Trenza as soon as the consul was gone. There was no way we could attack without half the shells falling on the American side.

''Maybe Pacotas will surrender without a fight,'' he answered.

But the commander of the Pacotas garrison was perfectly well aware of the fix we were in and refused to surrender.

We sent Juan Paredes, that Hero of Mexican Aviation, to make a reconnaissance flight in the Curtiss we'd brought along on our train for this very purpose. The situation was a delicate one and we had to know exactly where the enemy's defenses were located.

He brought back some very bad news. The defense positions were set up in a semicircle on the far side of the railroad station, very close to the river, and right behind them was . . . General Pershing.

I was about to suggest that we take our business elsewhere when Benítez had another of his brilliant ideas.

We would load a railroad car with dynamite, tow it up to the top of the hill eight kilometers outside the town, and let it go from there. The tracks sloped downward all the way from there to the station, and we figured the car would gather enough speed to run straight into the stationmaster's office and blow all the troops to Kingdom Come, yet cause not one bit of damage to American property.

The plan received our whole-hearted, unanimous approval and, since there was no time to spare, we set to work immediately.

Chapter XVI

As the vehicle to be used in our delicate mission, we chose a dining car that had seen better days. It took us all night to get the dynamite and prepare the detonators, and the sun was coming up by the time a locomotive was brought and hitched up to the diner. Benítez and I climbed aboard with a motorman and a stoker. When I gave the command to move out, the wheels began to move very slowly, then gradually picked up speed. The uphill climb started near Kilometer 10.* I was afraid somebody might start shooting at us (and our hundreds of pounds of dynamite), but there was no one in sight. It was drizzling.

When we reached the top of the hill, we stopped the engine, disconnected the diner, got behind it and pushed it a few meters; at last it started to coast downhill. It was moving quite fast by the time it disappeared around a curve.

We looked at our watches and waited.

Nothing happened. There was no explosion.

We went back to camp. Germán Trenza and the Jinx were waiting for me.

"What happened?" Trenza asked. "Why didn't it blow up?"

"I have no idea," I admitted.

---

* Kilometer numbers specify the distance from Pacotas.

We sent a cavalry squadron back along the tracks to investigate.

The suspense was awful. We were all anxious to get this whole business over and done with. We wanted to move—forward or back—but move! Everything was all set for the "lightning maneuver" we'd planned so carefully, the attack we'd have launched if the Americans hadn't butted in. And now we were stymied, so to speak, and to make matters worse, we didn't know what had become of our rail car and our dynamite.

It was nearly noon when the squadron returned and reported that the car was standing at Kilometer 4½.

I immediately hopped onto the locomotive, which had been kept in readiness and still had a full head of steam. Benítez got on too.

"Take us to Kilometer Four and a half," I ordered the motorman.

There it was, just as they'd told us it would be, standing at Kilometer 4½. I've never been able to figure out what made it stop there because the tracks still sloped downhill and there were no obstacles or anything.

"It wasn't going fast enough," Benítez decided. "Let's push it some more."

I said no because I didn't want to crash into the stationmaster's office—diner, dynamite, and all.

We hooked up the car again and towed it back to Kilometer 8 and the top of the hill. We stopped. The stoker unhitched the car.

"Okay, let's go! Full speed to Kilometer Six!"

And off we went, scared stiff, pushing the diner as fast as the engine would go (downhill too) with a ton of dynamite right under our noses.

When we passed Kilometer 7, I told the motorman to slow down.

The diner pulled away from us and raced ahead.

We couldn't hear a thing above the noise of the engine, so we couldn't be sure if there'd been an explosion or not. We came to a stop.

"There should be a big bang!" Benítez said.

So we stood there at Kilometer 6, not knowing what to do and unable to see anything because the tracks curved out of sight.

I didn't want to press my luck because I knew that sooner or later we'd run into enemy advance guards; on the other hand, I hated the idea of going back to camp. I'd only have to send out another squadron to investigate and all that. It would mean another whole day wasted.

"Why don't we go just as far as the next curve?" Benítez pleaded.

"Are you sure you didn't hear anything?" I asked the two railroad men, not wanting to get any closer to the enemy than absolutely necessary.

"Not a thing," they replied.

"Well, all right then, let's go. But take it easy!"

So we started moving very slowly and when we came around the curve, we saw the car. It was standing at Kilometer 4½ again!

We all cursed.

We pulled up to the diner and hooked it to our engine very cautiously.

"Let's go back to camp. Maybe we'll think of something else we can do," I said. But Benítez wanted to give it one more try.

"We could let the whole thing go, locomotive and all! We can walk back," he suggested.

"Oh, no! In the first place, with the locomotive running, there's a chance it might keep going all the way over to the American side, and in the second place, I don't want to waste an engine, because we don't have any to spare,'' I told him.

He was still convinced his invention would work, but I ordered our return to camp, the diner in tow.

''We have to consult the others,'' I said, to end all argument.

''Couldn't we push it a little more? Just to Kilometer Three, General.''

I must confess that the main reason I wanted to get back to camp was that I was tired of fooling around with the dynamite this way and that. *If they want to push it to Kilometer 3,* I thought to myself, *somebody else can do it.*

So we headed back to camp.

I gave orders for the diner to be left on the most remote siding because I didn't want to be blown to bits in case it should suddenly decide to explode.

At this rate, we'll be here the rest of our lives, I thought. Besides, none of all this would have been necessary if the Jinx had done his job. From the very outset we should have sent him somewhere else, to do something less important. He always had such rotten luck.

That afternoon we held a staff meeting.

''I could drop a few bombs,'' Juan Paredes offered.

''Too bad we don't have any to drop,'' Germán reminded him.

I thought we should go back to Cuévano and from there march on Mexico City; Odilón Rendón wanted to attack Piedras Negras, just this side of the border from Eagle Pass, Texas.

''If we beat Macedonio Gálvez, the *americanos* will be willing enough to open up the border to us.''

The Jinx had nothing to say; Trenza had bawled him out.

Benítez still had faith in the dynamite.

"We could send it off with the engine running," he persisted.

"You can send it off any way you please," I said abruptly, "but you'll have to do it yourselves." And then it occurred to me that the best idea might be to let it go with the Jinx on board. Maybe he'd take his bad luck with him. But I didn't suggest this out loud.

We were still arguing, splitting hairs, getting crankier by the minute, when our telegraph operator rushed in.

"There's a telegram for you, General, from our guard at the Azuela Station," he announced. He handed Trenza a paper with the following message:

TRAIN PASSED THROUGH THIS DEPOT STOP REFUSED TO IDENTIFY ITSELF STOP TRAVELING NORTHWARD.

"Have it stopped when it reaches Noria," Germán instructed. Then he turned to us and said, "We'll pick up where we left off in the morning. We're all on edge and getting nowhere."

And he got up and went off to relax (with Camila, who never left his side). The rest of us went to sleep.

Chapter XVII

I'd been assigned one of the compartments in the Pullman car reserved for the commanders. It had been a long, hard day, and I was sleeping soundly when Germán Trenza came to shake me awake.

"We just got word from Noria that Valdivia is on that train."

"Which train?" I asked, because I'd forgotten about the telegram.

Of course, as soon as I was fully awake, I realized that something very peculiar was going on.

"What's Valdivia coming here for?"

"We can ask him that when he gets here; that should be in half an hour. Get dressed." Saying this, Trenza went away to do likewise; he was in his underwear.

Then he came tiptoeing back.

"Don't let anyone hear you; there may be bad news."

We got out of the car and went to the tent where the aides were quartered and told them to saddle our horses.

The night was very dark because the sky was overcast; the ground was wet and muddy, but at least it wasn't raining. We sent for the officer of the guard.

"Notify the sentries that General Arroyo and I are going out; tell them not to shoot us," Trenza instructed him.

They brought our horses. We mounted and rode south about three kilometers along the railroad ties and came to the guardpost. When we could hear the train coming, Trenza gave orders for a lantern to be lit and placed on the tracks. Then the headlight appeared in the distance. It grew larger and larger and, finally, the train ground to a halt with a loud hiss and screech.

We realized that the people on the train were scared.

"Who goes there?" a voice called from the cab.

"Our Nation and Revolutionary Restoration," Trenza chanted. This was the password we'd decided on.

"General Valdivia is on this train."

"We know it. Tell him Trenza and Arroyo are here to see him."

Several men had climbed off the train during this exchange. One of them came closer, wrapped in a blanket. It was Anastasio Rodríguez.

"What's going on, Anastasio?" we asked him.

"Come with me," was his brief reply.

We followed him. There was a dining car and two stockcars filled with sleeping soldiers. Juan Valdivia was standing on the platform of the diner, wearing a knitted cap, a muffler, and a white sweater. He embraced us so emotionally that we knew that something very bad must have happened.

"We've been betrayed," he told us, almost sobbing.

"Come on, now, tell us about it," Trenza urged. We went into the car and sat down at the table.

What Juan Valdivia told us is possibly one of the most shameful episodes in the history of the Mexican Army.

As agreed, Valdivia had spent the first days after our departure from Cuévano fortifying the outlying districts. The reports received from the two expeditionary forces were inconclusive; neither of the missions had been carried out.

The Chameleon hadn't been able to find Fatty Artajo, and we hadn't taken Pacotas. On the other hand, he'd learned that Macedonio Gálvez's plans were coming along beautifully. His column had already left Celaya and was on its way to attack the Restoration forces.

"All this," Juan Valdivia told us, "created a tense atmosphere among the troops." They were beginning to desert. Well, now, all my years of experience in the army have taught me that soldiers don't desert because reports are inconclusive and danger is on the way, unless they're convinced (either by evidence or intuition) that they're being led by a bungler. The fact that Juan Valdivia was incompetent has been fully demonstrated. What I can't understand is not that the troops realized he was a bungler, but that *we* hadn't discovered it before we made him Commander in Chief of the East Army of the Restoration Forces.

So this was the situation Valdivia was up against: His men were deserting and, besides, Chávez wanted to go back home to Apapátaro, and Cenón Hurtado was getting sulkier by the day. And what was the brilliant idea suggested by this big jackass (Juan Valdivia)? "A little game" in a railroad car. (When I say "game" I mean [the gathering of several persons for the purpose of engaging in] games of chance.) And that's what they did; they sat and played cards, then played cards some more: Valdivia, Anastasio Rodríguez, Horacio Flores, and some other officers.

All of a sudden, without warning, a spray of bullets crashed through the windows of the dining car and sent them scrambling under the tables. They emerged only long enough to tell the motorman of a passing locomotive hauling two carloads of marijuana-drugged soldiers to hitch up their diner and take them to the north.

* * *

Trenza and I listened to Juan Valdivia, who told us all this with no apology and never even realizing that one was called for. To this day nobody knows who shot at them or why, because not one of the gamblers thought of trying to find out what was going on and whether it could be controlled (or if it did occur to them, they didn't have the guts to do anything about it).

Chávez went over to the government's side when he learned that Macedonio Gálvez was moving in, because he knew our own campaign was going sour. But we'll never know just how hopeless the situation was because no one made an effort to save it. Whoever shot at that dining car won the easiest battle in history. In one night we lost seven thousand men and the big, rich city of Cuévano. We lost Apapátaro too, because the next day Cenón Hurtado, who'd been left in charge there, made a statement that he was on the side of Eulalio Pérez and the "Legitimate Authorities." He was rewarded with a little thirty-five-thousand-acre ranch.

On the other hand, all Trenza and I got that night was an incompetent general with no army. After all our victories, won with fire and blood, the only thing he'd salvaged was his own hide, something we had no use for except maybe to fill it with holes, because no one has ever more richly deserved a quick trial and firing squad. We didn't pursue the idea because it was written that everything we'd do from that day forward would be a mistake.

It was a mistake not to get rid of Valdivia; it was a mistake to abandon the attack on Pacotas and to move away from the border, because that was when we should have crossed into the United States and asked for political asylum; it was also a mistake to retreat to Ciudad Rodríguez, a railroad junction in the middle of a desert. Although the Chameleon found us there and Fatty Artajo would have found us there if he'd taken the trouble to look, by the end of the month we were cornered, watching and waiting for an army to come riding in on enemy trains, along the four sets of tracks that ran into Ciudad Rodríguez, to finish us off.

Chapter XVIII

What made us decide to quarter our cavalry brigade at the Hacienda Santa Ana? I really don't know. Of all the places we might have picked for our troops, this was undoubtedly the worst possible choice. At the time, however, not only did I propose this arrangement, but I accepted command of the brigade.

It is true that Santa Ana offered an excellent observation post; it's true that the house provided comfortable lodgings for our three regiments; it's also true that Mrs. Ellen Goo, the owner, was a wonderful hostess. But why send a thousand men there, if all we needed were some good field glasses and a telephone?

Unwise as the choice may have been, however, Germán Trenza's statements to the *Heraldo de León* are outrageous lies. I didn't suggest setting up the brigade at Santa Ana ". . . only as á pretext to spend a few days with Ellen Goo . . ." because if my intentions toward the aforementioned lady had been dishonorable, I wouldn't have needed the brigade or anything else, because we have always been, and are to this day, very close friends. At my slightest insinuation, she would have given me anything my heart desired. I went to Santa Ana because, as I've already said, everything we did in those days turned out to be a mistake.

At any rate, there we were—Odilón Rendón, Anastasio, and I—like Hannibal at Capua; we played poker with Ellen

Goo day and night. On August 25 at twelve noon they came
to tell us that Macedonio's advance cavalry had just been
spotted. Aware that our inactivity was about to come to an
end and that the culminating moment of the campaign was at
hand, we left the card table and rushed to the observation
post.

We saw a force of some four squadrons riding toward
Ciudad Rodríguez beside the Cuévano tracks. After giving
the appropriate orders, I returned to the Hacienda and, even
as I was cranking the telephone, the bugles were sounding
the alert.

"We've lost all communication to the south, General,"
the operator informed me.

I realized that Macedonio's men had already cut the lines.

"Get me our headquarters in Ciudad Rodríguez," I ordered. There was some static and then a voice came on the
line:

"General Headquarters."

"How many times do I have to tell you to find out who's
calling first?" I shouted in a fury. They always forgot to ask
me to identify myself.

"Two hundred twenty-six," was the reply.

"Three hundred forty-two," I said. We had a code that
nobody who wasn't in on the secret could possibly decipher.
It changed with each telephone call. I asked to speak to Valdivia, but he wasn't there. Trenza came to answer.

"They're coming!" I told him.

The situation was dangerous, but not desperate. We were
facing an enemy greatly superior in number and equipment
and we knew that the only way we could beat them was by
acting without delay and attacking before they had a chance
to close ranks and take their positions. Before I hung up,
Anastasio came to tell me that Macedonio's trains had been
sighted.

"Attack with your cavalry," Trenza instructed me when he heard this latest information, and he promised he'd load our troops onto our trains and come to my aid as soon as he could.

Trenza's promise was responsible for what happened next. Within two hours I was attacking Macedonio Gálvez's forces and, since Trenza didn't show up with the infantry, it wasn't long before I was retreating with heavy losses. The newspapers called this unimportant skirmish a "great defeat." It's true that I retreated to Santa Ana somewhat hastily; it's true that we suffered more than a hundred casualties, counting dead, wounded, prisoners, and deserters; it's even true that we had to pull out of the Hacienda Santa Ana that same night, but it was no great defeat. What's more, it wasn't my fault!

As soon as we got back to Santa Ana, we got busy setting up our defense positions, in case they decided to come after us. Germán Trenza drove up in an automobile, raising a cloud of dust.

He launched into a string of insults without even saying hello.

"It's all your fault that everything went to who-knows-where!" he shouted.

"It's yours, you miserable so-and-so!" I snapped back.

We exchanged curses for a while. When we calmed down, we discovered that something completely unheard of had happened. After we'd agreed on the telephone that Trenza would come to our assistance along the railroad line toward Cuévano, another telephone call was received at our General Headquarters. It was undoubtedly made by the enemy, who had, also undoubtedly, intercepted our previous conversation and, thanks to the carelessness of our operators who invariably forgot to identify the caller, told Trenza a lie in that second conversation: that the orders had been countermanded and that the attack would be on the line toward Monterrey. So while I was battling bravely, if futilely, against Macedonio's advance troops, Germán Trenza was taking a ride with three thousand men—in the wrong direction, where, needless to say, he didn't run into a living soul.

"How many times have I told them not to forget to identify the caller?" I demanded, angrier than ever. "If we took the time and trouble to make up a code, it's supposed to be used!"

Germán was so ashamed of having been made to look the fool that he remained silent.

"You'd better come back with me," he said after a while. "We're going to have to defend Ciudad Rodríguez."

He was right. There was no longer any point in keeping the cavalry at Santa Ana. The enemy was off the trains and ready for combat. We were outnumbered; the best we could do was defend Ciudad Rodríguez and hold out as long as we could, in the hope that Fatty Artajo would show up soon with his seven thousand men and four artillery regiments.

When Germán and I parted, we were sad but reconciled. He went back to Ciudad Rodríguez in his automobile and I went to the hacienda to make arrangements for our departure and to say good-bye to Mrs. Ellen Goo.

Chapter XIX

I rode into Ciudad Rodríguez at midnight; my cavalry brigade was somewhat smaller than it had been when we set out because Odilón Rendón got lost in the dark with a whole regiment. At first we thought he'd taken a short cut, but we finally realized he'd gone over to the enemy. I can't blame him. I might have been tempted to do the same thing if I weren't a man of integrity.

We couldn't find any place to quarter the troops, who finally ended up sleeping in the town's main square. Anastasio and I went to the Rodríguez Hotel, where General Headquarters had been installed.

Valdivia, Trenza, the Chameleon, and the Jinx were sitting in the dining room with long faces, trying to figure out how to win a battle that was already as far beyond hope as my sainted mother. I told them so.

"Let's go to the border and ask for political asylum!"

But everyone still thought that Fatty Artajo would appear with his seven thousand men and his four artillery regiments. Well, everyone except the Chameleon. He didn't believe in anything.

"If I were in Fatty's boots, I'd stay away from a trap like this," he said, and he was right.

In reply, Valdivia said a lot of things about brotherhood, loyalty, and comradeship. (As if he knew the first thing

about friendship!) At any rate, they still had faith in Fatty
Artajo. The Chameleon and I didn't.

They showed me a map of the city's defenses.

"They're no good," I told them.

Valdivia was furious.

"What do you mean, they're no good? You haven't even
seen them!"

It's really very simple. When you fortify a city, you have
to dig your trenches outside, around all the buildings and
houses, not in the middle. If the enemy occupies any of the
houses outside the line of trenches, you're practically making yourself a target in a shooting gallery. We all know that.
I told them so.

"But if we put them where they're supposed to be,"
Germán Trenza explained, "the trenches would be too long
and we wouldn't have enough men to fill them."

"It would still be better to have an undermanned trench
than to give the enemy cover right in front of you to shoot
from!" I pointed out. The Chameleon knew I was right and
so, at heart, did Germán Trenza. Valdivia was the only one
who was perfectly satisfied with the planned defenses.

"I ordered them that way," he said, as if that made it any
more sensible.

"We could demolish these houses," suggested Trenza,
pointing to the ones left outside the defense line. But we all
knew there wasn't enough time for demolitions—or for anything else.

"Let's head for the border," I urged again, but nobody
paid the slightest attention to me.

We couldn't agree on anything—as usual. We adjourned
the meeting not because we'd finished our business or made
any decisions, but because we were very tired.

On our way out, the Chameleon drew me aside.

"This fool Valdivia is messing everything up," he whispered, though in more vulgar words.

I told him he'd taken the words out of my mouth.

"We ought to get rid of him—for the sake of the Revolution, of course," he added.

I agreed.

Just then Trenza joined us. We told him what we'd been talking about because we knew he shared our opinion of Valdivia.

"Let's execute him," he proposed. "We've had enough of his blunders!"

"We'd get into a lot of trouble, and don't forget, he was our own candidate. I have a better idea," said the Chameleon, and then he explained his diabolic plan:

"Let's send him to look for Fatty Artajo. We'll send him with Juan Paredes in the airplane. If he finds Fatty and the reinforcements reach us in time, so much the better. If he doesn't, at least we'll have gotten him out of our hair."

We thought it was a marvelous idea.

At eight the next morning, we held another meeting and named Valdivia Commander in Chief of the West Army (Fatty Artajo's). By nine we were seeing him off.

"Don't worry, boys," Valdivia assured us. "I'll come to your rescue just as soon as I can."

With these words, he got into the Curtiss, where Juan Paredes (Hero of Mexican Aviation) was already waiting. They got off the ground without mishap and soon disappeared into the clouded August sky. That was the last anyone ever saw of them because, to this day, there's been no sign of them—or their remains.

While this was happening, five thousand men arrived from Monterrey to attack us.

Unfortunately, the damage had already been done, thanks to Juan Valdivia's incompetence. The next day, after a very brief skirmish, the enemy took the outlying houses; from these ideal vantage points they shot at us like sitting ducks and caused a great many casualties.

"We've got to do something," Trenza said at the meeting we held after this sad occurrence.

I hated to risk my troops, our only reserve, but there was no other choice.

"If you give me artillery cover, I'll try to get them out."

Benítez was enthusiastic and, at ten o'clock, he started to shell the houses; then the infantry's machine guns opened fire; the barrage was so thick, the enemy must have been knocked flat. After a quarter of an hour, the shooting stopped and my cavalry charged, yelling at the top of their lungs. They weren't expecting us, and the enemy soldiers poured out of their hiding places like scared rabbits. We chased them to the outskirts of town and stopped just short of their second firing line. Then we withdrew in victory.

Our mission was accomplished! Our infantry now occupied every last house in the town. During this action, my troops took fourteen prisoners and, when we got back to the town square, I turned them over to the Jinx, who was in charge of the prison.

Then I went to the hotel and told my aide to cook me a steak because the battle had whetted my appetite. I heard some shots being fired across the square. I was eating the aforementioned steak when a captain came running to tell me that the Jinx was shooting all the prisoners. I jumped up from the table angrily. When you're losing a war, you can't afford to be cruel to prisoners. By the time I got to the jail, they were all dead.

"I didn't have anybody to guard them," the Jinx explained.

"Full responsibility for this war crime rests on your

shoulders," I told him; then I went to look for Trenza, who was at the station.

"We'll have to hold a court-martial," he decided, when I told him what had happened.

And we held one. With a notary public to sign the transcript and everything, to show that it had been a fair trial, that we'd had no part in executing prisoners of war, and that we'd promptly punished the guilty party.

The Chameleon presided. The court found the Jinx guilty and sentenced him to be stripped of rank and executed.

We took him to the courtyard at once. I ripped off all his insignia and Benítez commanded the firing squad. By four that afternoon, our good friend Canalejo, the Jinx of the Mexican Army, was resting in his grave.

"Maybe now our luck will take a turn for the better," Trenza hoped, but no sooner were these words out of his mouth than a counterattack ousted our men from the houses we'd just regained.

Everything was quiet that night, but we still lost two hundred men; they deserted to the enemy.

"Let's go to the border!" I said the following day at our meeting.

By then, nobody really believed that Fatty Artajo would ever show up with his seven thousand men and four artillery regiments.

"All right," Trenza agreed. "Let's make our plans."

I got the worst job, as usual. The withdrawal was to begin at eight that night. First the armored railcar would move out with the artillery, under Benítez; then the Chameleon and Trenza would each take a car with infantry troops. Anastasio and I were assigned to hold out with the cavalry as long as we could and then withdraw at our discretion; in other words, we were on our own.

That night my men held their positions and returned the

enemy fire, which got heavier by the minute. I think they'd guessed that we were about to try to get away.

At three in the morning, I told Anastasio to take one of our two remaining regiments and leave.

"We'll meet at the canyon," I told him.

He and his men rode away. I walked through the town; it was deserted except for the wounded, who were lying in the main square, tended by our doctor.

"Good luck," I wished him. Later he was executed in reprisal for the prisoners shot by the Jinx.

From there I went to the railroad station and ordered that all our baggage be burned. There was quite a big pile of it.

Finally, I told my men to abandon their posts. We got under way near dawn.

We were riding down the road when suddenly we heard a terrible explosion from the direction of the railroad tracks. In a burst of comradeship I can't explain to this day, I decided to take the time to investigate. Leaving the road, we galloped to the top of a rise; from there we saw a railcar in flames!

We rode down to the tracks. What a mess!

Benítez had become so attached to his diner loaded with dynamite that he dragged it around wherever he went. It had exploded. Nobody knows why. The two carloads of ammunition blew up with it; so did all our guns; so, of course, did all the occupants of the train, including Benítez, our ingenious inventor, who had rendered such invaluable service. He would have had a brilliant military career and a great future if he hadn't joined up with us.

But losing all our artillery and ammunition wasn't the worst of it; the tracks were blocked and the two trainloads of infantry couldn't get through. Now they'd have to retreat on foot.

"I almost feel like surrendering," Trenza told me when I

found him. I know that hurt him because he'd been a coura-
geous officer who'd never given up. But Camila was preg-
nant and couldn't walk.

The Chameleon talked him out of it.

"What do you want to stay for, Germán? To be stood up
against a wall and shot?"

I got him some horses and we went on our way slowly.

At four in the afternoon, the enemy was practically on top
of us—and shooting. I led a charge, hoping to scare them
away, but it didn't work.

That night I moved the cavalry well to the rear, to protect
the retreating infantry. When it was time to resume march
and I rode up to join them, nobody was left except Germán
Trenza, the Chameleon, Camila, and two aides. The infantry had scattered during the night.

"They deserted," Trenza explained.

"I don't blame them," I remarked.

We reached the canyon at sunset. Our entire force had
been reduced to one scant squadron.

Chapter XX

Anastasio and the twelve men he'd managed to salvage from the stampede were entrenched in the peaks overlooking the entrance to the canyon.

We held a meeting.

Anastasio and Horacio Flores were in favor of surrendering.

"We've lost the war. Why keep on fighting?" Anastasio said.

"To keep from getting shot," the Chameleon replied. Trenza and I agreed with him.

Horacio Flores tried to convince us that the worst they could do to us was to deport us.

"If it's going to be our destiny to spend the rest of our days in the United States anyway," I said, "it would be much better to go of our own free will and not go through the shame of being accused of high treason and all that." I might as well have saved my breath because we never came to any agreement in that meeting. Anastasio and Horacio Flores finally went off to look for somebody to surrender to. Trenza, the Chameleon, and I drew lots to see which of us would stay behind at the canyon to slow down the enemy while the others headed for the border. I lost.

At dawn, when they were ready to go, my companions took their leave of me as if I were a great hero. They were giving me up for dead. So was I.

When they rode out of the canyon on horses that could barely stand, a squad I'd sent to look for supplies came back with three cows they'd stolen. It was our first taste of food since we'd left Ciudad Rodríguez.

After our meal, I ordered them to form ranks.

"If any of you want to leave, you'd better go now."

Nobody went. If they were going to fall into the hands of the enemy, they wanted to do it in the company of a general; they didn't realize that I'd be the first one to be executed.

I divided up the money I had left; they decided to bury their shares so it wouldn't be taken from them when we were captured. Then I reviewed my troops: We had twenty men and two machine guns, with enough ammunition to hold out for about two hours, if we used it sparingly.

We should have gotten out of here when Trenza and the Chameleon did, I thought to myself.

When the enemy column appeared that afternoon, we fought courageously, but our ammunition ran out before sunset. Then we took out a white rag. They took one out too. I left my shelter and walked toward the enemy, fully expecting to be shot down. Fortunately, I wasn't.

They led me to their commander, who had once been my companion in arms. We embraced affectionately.

"Lupe!" he said. "I'm so glad to see you!"

Sure, you're glad to see me . ... to see me beaten, broken, done for, I thought.

"I'm turning myself in," I said, "but don't shoot my boys."

"Of course we won't," he answered. "You have my word that nothing will happen to them."

And nothing did happen to them. They spent only five years in a military prison.

I was taken to Ciudad Rodríguez.

"There's going to be a court-martial," the commander whispered as he handed me over at the guardhouse. He didn't have to tell me that. I'd been expecting it.

When I got inside the jail, I found Anastasio and Horacio Flores.

"They're going to shoot us in the morning," Anastasio announced as I entered the cell.

I embraced him, feeling sorry for him because he'd let his last chance to escape go by, and all because he'd believed everything Horacio Flores told him. It was only fair that Horacio was going to have to pay the same penalty for his optimism.

They were led before the firing squad at dawn the next day. I was given some breakfast, then escorted to the Rodríguez Hotel. The hearing was to take place in the dining room.

The minute I walked in, I could see that it was hopeless and that I was as good as executed. I knew them all: the prosecutor had a reputation for cleverness; the defender, for stupidity.

I asked permission to speak.

"I refuse to be represented by this defense counsel or any other. This trial is a hoax! You can say and do whatever you wish, but I refuse to take part in these proceedings." Having said this, I sat down, closed my mouth, and didn't open it again during the three hours the farce lasted.

The witnesses were there in full force: Cenón Hurtado, General Chávez, Governor Virgilio Urquiza, Father Jorge, the bank manager, two rich men from Apapátaro, the widow of one of the people we'd shot at Cuévano, and a few others. They threw the book at me; the charges were treason against the Nation, violation of the Constitution, insubordination, homicide, perjury, fraud, contributing to the delinquency of minors, smuggling, white-slave traffic—they even said I was a *Cristero*.

"I'm sorry, Lupe," the presiding officer told me when it was over, "but I received orders direct from the President of the Republic that it had to be this way."

"Don't worry about it," I replied. "I understand how those things are. No hard feelings."

And, come to think of it, I really didn't have any hard feelings.

The court placed me under the custody of the garrison commander, who was Macedonio Gálvez. An escort took me to the guardhouse, where I was locked in a cell.

When the officer of the guard came to inquire about my last request, I told him I wanted the latest newspaper and a bottle of Martell cognac.

Later, leafing through the papers, I learned that that so-and-so Fatty Artajo had stayed where he was and never even tried to come to help us. "His patriotic attitude," according to the papers, had been "one of the principal factors which made it possible to restore peace to the Nation." Artajo had been the Joker in our case (there had been one in the case of the unfortunate General Serrano too): the conspirator who vanishes on the day of the uprising and takes a big piece of the army with him. Then I realized, with great sadness, that we'd all been the toys of Vidal Sánchez. There weren't very many true revolutionaries anymore, just as he'd said; he wanted even fewer.

I finished my bottle of Martell and prepared to sleep away the remaining hours of my life. The cell door opened to admit Macedonio Gálvez.

"You know I have orders to execute you?" he asked. He was gloating. I didn't care anymore. "But I'm not going to do it. Because when I was so [here he used a word I cannot repeat], you invited me to lunch and gave me your pistol so I could pawn it.'' This last, needless to say, was an outra-geous lie. He stole my pearl-handled gun and I did everything I could to get him caught and executed. So while I'm grateful to Macedonio Gálvez for neglecting his duty and not having me shot, I want to set the record straight: I never gave him my gun. He stole it.

Of course, at that moment, I wasn't about to contradict him.

Epilogue

The corpse whose photograph was printed in the papers the next day belonged to a butcher they say looked a lot like me.

I joined Matilde and the children in San Antonio, Texas, where I spent eight of the most boring years of my existence. Vidal Sánchez and Eulalio Pérez were eventually deported from Mexico, and the survivors of the Revolution of 1929—Germán Trenza, the Chameleon, and I—returned to a hero's welcome. Trenza took up farming, the Chameleon went into politics, and I take care of my business and my family. We're doing pretty well.